Flour Babies

by
Anne Fine

Published by
Bantam Doubleday Dell Books for Young Readers
a division of
Bantam Doubleday Dell Publishing Group, Inc.
1540 Broadway
New York, New York 10036

The trademark Laurel-Leaf® is registered in the U.S. Patent
and Trademark Office.
The trademark Dell® is registered in the U.S. Patent
and Trademark Office.

ISBN: 0-440-21941-8

RL: 5.8

Reprinted by arrangement with Little, Brown and Company

Printed in the United States of America

November 1995

21 20 19 18 17 16 15 14 13

To every thing there is a season,
    and a time to every purpose under the heaven.

                                      Ecclesiastes 3:1

Flour Babies

CHAPTER 1

Mr. Cassidy swung his legs to and fro under the desk and raised his voice over the waves of bad-tempered muttering.

"Don't worry if you feel you can't give this your full attention now, Room 8," he said to his new class. "I'll be delighted to go over it again during your break-time."

Some of them visibly made a little more of an effort. A few pens were pulled out of a few mouths. One or two of the boys dragged their attention back from the riveting sight of the janitor outside by the gate painting large white numbers on the St. Boniface School's trash cans. But, on the whole, the improvement was pitiful. Half of them looked as if they'd left their brains at home. The other half looked as if they didn't have any.

This year's Room 8. What a pack! Mr. Cassidy knew most of them well enough already — the Sads and the Bads, the ones who had been despaired of most loudly and often in the teachers' room over the last couple of years. Anyone halfway normal (these were called the Lads) had been snatched up, as usual, by Mr. Hoover or Mr. Stoutamire. And Dr. Devoy always took all the Brains. So far, no one had ever ended up in Room 8 by accident.

The only boy new to the school — what was his name, Martin Simon? — was sitting reading quietly at the back. Mr. Cassidy cheered up a bit. That was a start, then. One of them could read. He must have had worse classes in his time.

"Buck up, boys," he told them. "This shouldn't take all day. I'll run through the choices one last time, and then you'll have to vote. You can keep on eating your ballot paper, George O'Rourke, but I'm not giving you another. Now pay attention, everyone."

Shifting his vast bottom around, he tapped the blackboard on which, five minutes earlier, he'd written the options Dr. Devoy had given the class for their contribution to the school Science Fair,

> textiles
> nutrition
> home economics
> child development
> consumer studies

reciting them aloud again for those who had trouble with reading.

A swell of grumbling rose over the fidgets and whispers and shuffling feet, and the creak of chairs being tipped back dangerously on two of their four legs.

"It isn't fair, Mr. Cassidy."

"Boring!"

"You can't call all of those Science. It's not right."

"I don't even know what half of them *mean*."

To oblige Spike Moranis, Mr. Cassidy read them off again, this time translating as he went along.

> sewing
> food
> housekeeping
> babies and so forth
> thrift

Spike Moranis was as baffled as ever.

"Frift? What's frift?"

Mr. Cassidy chose to ignore him.

"For God's sake, boys," he said. "Pull yourselves together. I know most of you have the boredom thresholds of brain-damaged gnats, but surely one of these topics must interest you more than the others. Whichever it is, copy it down on the paper. And do try to get the letters more or less in the right order, Spike Moranis, so I can read it. I'm coming around now to collect them."

Another mutinous wave rose up to greet him.

"Stupid!"

"Just trying to pick on us . . ."

"Sewing! Housekeeping!"

"Excuse me. We're Table 14 in the Science Fair. Come and look at our nice sewed-on buttons."

"So interesting. Oh, yes!"

"I bet you've never seen a sewed-on button before."

"What's the point of doing things if *anyone* can do them?"

"Frift!"

It was Tyrone Schumaker who voiced the general complaint in the most coherent fashion.

"It isn't fair. They're not *real* science, are they? None of them. Why can't we do the exploding custard cans?"

Instantly, it was as if all of them had been let out of a cage.

"Yeah! They were great!"

"The *best!*"

"Hooper's brother nearly burned his hand off."

"Chop lost an eyebrow."

"Grew back different."

Rick Tullis was leaning so far over his desk, it was likely to topple over.

"Or making soap, sir!"

"Yes! The Soap Factory!"

"Fuller ate his lump for a dare."

"Sick *eight times.*"

"We had a good laugh."

"Should have seen his face. Pale as a maggot!"

At this, Philip Brewster unleashed a fresh hue and cry around the room.

"Yes! Maggots!"

"Maggot Farm!"

"Yes! Why can't we do the Maggot Farm?"

"There was one last year. And the year before."

"My mom wouldn't even *look* at it. She said it was disgusting."

"That bully Fletcher was put in charge of running it."

"He practically had the maggots *trained* by the last day!"

Mr. Cassidy shook his head. It saddened him to have to dampen enthusiasm in any educational sphere. But facts are facts, especially in a school.

"May I invade your privacy for a moment, Tyrone, to ask if you happened to pass the Physics exam at the end of last term?"

Tyrone scowled horribly.

"No, I didn't, sir."

"And you, Rick. Did you pass Chemistry?"

Rick Tullis laughed. And so did everyone who'd been in last year's Chemistry class, along with Rick Tullis.

Mr. Cassidy turned to Philip, who was still bright-eyed at the thought of running the Maggot Farm.

"Philip? Any luck with Biology?"

Philip's expression soured.

"I didn't even bother to come in and take it, sir. No point."

Mr. Cassidy sighed.

"Well, there you have it in a nutshell, I'm afraid, Room 8. No one is here by accident."

At the back, suddenly, the new boy, Martin Simon, spoke up for the first time.

"I think I might be, sir."

But Mr. Cassidy, in full flow, ignored the inter-ruption.

"And therein lies the explanation of why, sadly, this class can't do the Exploding Custard Cans. In the absence of total confidence in your skills and com-mitment, Dr. Devoy has entrusted us only with nice, safe, and easy topics. Exploding Custard Cans have been reserved for those who passed Physics at the end of last year."

His eye roved over eighteen sullen faces and one rather intrigued one.

"Did *anyone* here pass Physics?"

The new boy raised his hand. Otherwise, no one stirred. And since Martin Simon was pretty well out of everyone's line of sight, in the back row, Mr. Cas-sidy chose not to let his one waving arm detract from the dramatics of the occasion.

"Anyone pass Chemistry?"

Again, Martin Simon's hand shot up in the air, to be totally ignored by Mr. Cassidy. Otherwise, noth-ing much happened.

"Good-bye, Soap Factory," Mr. Cassidy said. "How was our record in Biology? Anyone have any luck there?"

Martin Simon's arm waved, a lone reed over the silt of the rest of Room 8's academic hopes. For the third time, Mr. Cassidy pretended not to see it.

"So," he said flatly. "No Maggot Farm for us."

He spread his huge chalky hands.

"You can't say you weren't warned," he told them. "I get my coffee from the teachers' room. I have ears. Father Maguire, Mr. Reynolds, Mr. Dupasque, Miss Arnott. They all said it, more than once. '*I've warned them over and over*,' they all said. '*If they don't work, they'll end up in Room 8*.' And here you are."

"You can't help it if you're stupid," George O'Rourke argued.

"If you were stupid enough to be in this room, you'd be on a life-support system," said Mr. Cassidy tartly.

"So what are we doing here?"

Mr. Cassidy turned biblical.

"You're reaping as ye sowed. And, speaking of sewing, will you please get going and vote. What's it to be? Textiles, nutrition, home economics, child development, or consumer studies?"

"I'm not voting for none of them," said Warren Meyer. "They're all stupid."

Having a sneaking sympathy for this point of view, Mr. Cassidy said nothing. But when George O'Rourke added, "Girls' things, that's what they are!" he felt obliged to put his pupils right.

"Don't kid yourselves. While you guys are sitting here grumbling, girls all over the country are making soap, farming maggots, and exploding custard cans. They're studying Chemistry, Biology, and Physics. To the Victor the Spoils now. And they passed exams."

Then, tiring suddenly of the whole business, he started striding up and down the rows of desks, trying to coax them into voting. "Get *on* with it, Robin Delaney. Hurry up, Rick. What difference is it going to make to you? According to Miss Arnott, you hardly ever come to school anyway. Thank you, Tariq. Everyone look at Tariq. He is an example to you all. He chose. He wrote it down, not *neatly* exactly, but clearly enough to read. And now he's dropped his ballot slip in my tub. Thank you, Tariq. *Thank* you. And thank you, Henry. No need to *flick* it in. Thank you, Spike. Thank you. Thank you, Martin, and I hope you'll be very happy wi—"

Mr. Cassidy broke off. For it was clear the new boy wasn't even listening. As Mr. Cassidy's shadow fell across his desk, he'd simply pulled the forefinger of his right hand out of that ear for a moment, picked up his neatly written vote, and dropped it in the plastic tub. At no point had he so much as glanced up from his book.

Mr. Cassidy was mystified. Gently, he pried Martin Simon's fingers out of his ears, and asked him:

"What are you doing?"

Now the boy was equally confused.

"Reading, sir."

"Reading? Reading what?"

"Baudelaire."

Mr. Cassidy's eyes widened.

"*Baudelaire?*"

He glanced around the room, hoping for one mad

moment that none of his other pupils had heard the exchange. Fat chance of that. They were all sitting, ears on stalks.

"In French or English?" Mr. Cassidy asked, thinking to diffuse the tension with a joke.

Young Martin Simon flushed.

Mr. Cassidy swiveled the book around on the desk. "French!"

"Sorry," said Martin Simon automatically.

Mr. Cassidy sighed.

"So am I, lad. So am I."

There was a pause. Then Mr. Cassidy said:

"Well? What are you waiting for? Pack your book bag. Off you go."

Martin Simon looked up in astonishment.

"Go *where,* sir?"

"Anywhere. I should think a boy like you could take his pick. You could try Mr. Hoover's class. Or Mr. Stoutamire's. I bet either of them would be happy to have you."

"But *why?*"

Mr. Cassidy settled his huge rear end companionably on Martin Simon's desk. For an intelligent lad, he thought, he wasn't acting too bright.

"Look at it this way," he told him. "You can't stay here. For one thing, you can read. You'll be right out of place here from that alone. Then there's the other problem. You read French."

He waved a hand airily around the room, to draw in the others who were sitting there staring.

"I expect there'll be quite a lot of language in this classroom," he explained. "I, for one, have a temper. Then there's the colorful *patois* of our local housing project to be contended with. And Tariq here, I'm told, swears in three separate subcontinental dialects. But no one speaks French."

He shifted on the desk.

"No," he said. "I'm afraid you'll have to go."

A thought struck him.

"With all those science exams you passed, you could even try Dr. Devoy. He might take you."

At last Martin Simon seemed to grasp the point. Rising to his feet, he started shoveling the few possessions he'd unpacked back into his book bag.

Mr. Cassidy caught the rather regretful expression on the boy's face.

"I'm sorry about it too, son," he said. "But, believe me, it's for the best. You wouldn't fit in here. There's been some mistake."

Martin Simon nodded.

"Ask at the office," Mr. Cassidy advised, walking him to the door. "Tell them they've got it all wrong, and you can't come back here. I won't have you. You don't belong."

He saw him off on the long trek down the green corridor.

"Good-bye, son," he called out wistfully after him. "Good luck!"

He swung the door closed and turned to face the rest with iron determination.

"Right!" he said. "Put that scarf away, Tyrone. Are you eating, Luis Pereira? Spit it out in the wastebasket. Look how much time we've wasted. I warn you, I'm getting this finished before the bell rings."

With any other class, he might have managed it. But what with two of the tellers he chose not being all that good at counting, and the constant delays as people criticized each way of tallying ("You can't count Rick's vote, sir! He's never here!"), there wasn't time to get it done. Even before the third recount was complete, Robin Delaney and Wayne Driscoll were eyeing him with their imaginary stopwatches raised, and lips pursed around their nonexistent whistles.

It was almost Time . . .

Mr. Cassidy slid his vast bulk off the desk onto his feet, making the floor shake and the windows rattle.

"Hush up!" he bellowed, cutting directly through all the layers of noise at once. "That's it! I've had enough! The bell's about to ring, and we're wrapping this up one way or another. I warn you, Room 8, the very next boy responsible for any noise in this room — *any noise at all* — will have to dip his hand in this tub and take out a ballot slip, and whatever it says on that goes."

The silence was instant and total. High fliers they might not be, but every one of them was bright enough not to relish the idea of being blamed by all the rest for three solid weeks of work on some project cruelly designed by Dr. Devoy to bring out the latent interest of things like sewing or cooking or house-keeping.

It seemed no one dared breathe. Mr. Cassidy could even hear the warble of a songbird outside in the gutter.

Then, without warning, the spell broke.

The other side of the classroom door suddenly suffered the most tremendous thud. The doorknob rattled and the panels shook.

In walked a clumsy young giant.

A roar of approval greeted the newcomer's entrance.

"Yo, nitface!"

"Last one in class gets maimed!"

"Sime! Saved a place for you!"

"Found us finally, have you, you great banana!"

"Get a *brain*, Simon Martin!"

Simon Martin . . . Martin Simon . . . Of course.

Mr. Cassidy heaved himself back into his usual position on the desk. So there was the explanation. Simple enough. Mere clerical error.

Martin Simon . . . Simon Martin . . .

He let the flurry of excitement ride for a few moments longer.

"Where've you *been*, Sime?"

"Got stuck," declared the newcomer proudly. "In Dr. Devoy's class."

"Dr. Devoy's!"

Another roar of laughter, and even Mr. Cassidy had to smile, trying to picture this huge, strapping, and unthinking lad marooned among Dr. Devoy's keen and ambitious pupils.

"I told him I didn't *belong*. But would he listen? Not him. Not till that other earhole finally came along and rescued me. And even then —"

To cut off what was clearly all set to develop into a prolonged riff of resentment, Mr. Cassidy held the plastic tub of votes out toward his brand-new pupil.

"Pick one," he said.

Simon Martin's look of deep disgruntlement turned into one of even deeper suspicion.

"What is it for?"

"Just pick one." Mr. Cassidy sharpened the tone to an order. "Now."

Simon Martin reached in and picked the one that happened to be written most neatly.

"What does it say?"

The boy stared at it for a few moments. His massive caterpillar eyebrows crumpled in confusion as he struggled with Martin Simon's perfect handwriting. Then:

"Chile . . . chile . . . chile dev-lop-ment," he read aloud stumblingly.

"Development."

Mr. Cassidy managed to slide in the correction a split second before the explosion.

"That's *babies*, isn't it?"

"We're not doing *babies*, sir!"

"That *is* girls' stuff. It *is!*"

"I won't be coming in at all now! Not till it's all over, anyhow."

"I'm blaming you, Sime!"

"You can't call it *science*. It's just a great big *cheat!*"

"Pick again, Sime!"

Hastily, Mr. Cassidy upended the tub over the wastebasket. The remaining votes floated down to join whatever it was Luis Pereira had spat in earlier.

Mr. Cassidy flicked through the pages of Dr. Devoy's vast Science Fair memorandum. Oh, what a ghastly way to start the term! Why couldn't the man arrange things the way every other school did, and leave the great tribute to the wonders of science until the last couple of weeks before the holidays, when classes like this one could be left peaceably slacking? That was the trouble with enthusiasts, of course. They never allowed for other people's weaknesses.

Finding the right page at last, Mr. Cassidy raised his voice like someone announcing the winner of an Oscar, and declared solemnly:

"And the experiment Dr. Devoy has chosen for this topic is —"

He glanced around. He hadn't even said it yet, and already a sea of disgusted faces was staring back at him.

"Flour babies!"

Now scorn was supplanted by confusion.

"Sir?"

"Is that *flour* babies or *flower* babies?"

"They both sound weird to me."

"What *are* they?"

"Whatever they are, they don't sound much like real *science.*"

Secretly, that was what Mr. Cassidy thought. He glanced at the list again. Could it be a mistake? Another clerical error?

No. There it was, clear as paint.

Flour babies.

Right.

Mr. Cassidy slapped Dr. Devoy's memorandum down on the desk. Whatever they were, there was no time to read about them now. Already, Wayne Driscoll's cheeks were puffed to bursting, and he was waving his imaginary stopwatch about wildly.

And, sure enough, the bell rang.

Just one more short ritual to get through, and the lesson would be over. Who would be first today?

Billy Simms.

"Excuse me, Billy Simms. I don't remember anyone telling you this lesson was over. Back in your seat, please."

"But, sir! Sir! The bell's rung."

"That bell's for me, Billy. It is not for you."

His heart wasn't in it, though. No, not today. In fact, to get rid of them just a little bit sooner, he even stooped to pretending he hadn't seen Spike Moranis's bottom hovering an insolent ten inches clear of the chair, ready to make the big getaway.

"All right, Room 8. Off you go."

They hurled themselves at the door in a disorderly rabble, leaving him wondering.

Flour babies . . . What on earth?

CHAPTER 2

Simon Martin sprawled over the three chairs out-side the teachers' room door. He'd been sent there for being a nuisance at Morning Prayers. He'd only arrived four minutes earlier, and already he was bored halfway out of his skull. He'd tried whistling (and been told off for it by Miss Arnott on her way in). He'd tried tapping tunes with his feet (and been told off for it by Mr. Stoutamire on his way out). He'd even tried seeing how many different clicking noises he could make with his tongue (and been told off for it by Father Maguire as he walked past).

They'd left him no choice, really.

They couldn't expect him to sit there all day doing nothing.

When the next teacher came out, he'd give it a try.

The next teacher to come out was Mr. Dupasque. As the door swung behind him, Simon Martin sur-reptitiously shifted one of his quite enormous feet a couple of inches backward and used his heel to stop the door from closing properly.

It was their own fault. If they didn't want someone who had already been picked on in Assembly for no reason at all getting so bored he ended up listening to what they were saying, they should have left him alone while he was peacefully whistling and tapping and clicking.

Simon settled in for a good eavesdrop. In fact, if he turned his head to the right as if he were gazing down the corridor, he could even see a thin slice of teachers' room out of the corner of his eye. Across it, Old Hopalong was reeling, making one of his jumbo-sized fusses.

"I don't believe this," Mr. Cassidy was bellowing. "I cannot believe my *ears*. Are you seriously trying to tell me that these child development project things of yours are literally six pounds of plain white flour sewn into a burlap bag? And you intend to give one of these things to each of the maniacs in my class?"

"Not give, Howard. Lend."

"Give. Lend." Simon caught a brief glimpse of a slice of Mr. Cassidy's arms, thrown up in a gesture of despair. "With that pack of sociopaths, what difference does it make? No one in Room 8 could take care of a *stone* without cracking it. You can't expect six-pound bags of flour to survive!"

Through the gap, Simon saw a strip of Dr. Devoy's anxious face.

"Not six pounds, Howard. Three kilos. Now do try to set an example. Think in grams."

"I'll think how I damn well want, thank you,"

Simon overheard Mr. Cassidy growl. "And, frankly, I think you must be off your rocker. There are nineteen boys in Room 8 this term, you know. Nineteen times six is one hundred and twenty-three!"

"One hundred and fourteen," Dr. Devoy couldn't help correcting.

"*What?*"

Dr. Devoy mistook Mr. Cassidy's mixture of impatience and outrage for a sincere quest for mathematical enlightenment.

"I think you must have multiplied the nine by seven by mistake," he said. "It's the only rational explanation for that particular error."

What with all this fancy talk of numbers, Simon's attention was flagging. He was about to slide his foot forward and let the door close again, when another slice of Mr. Cassidy reeled into view, and he heard his class teacher howl.

"Hundred and this! Hundred and that! What does it matter? It's still over a hundred pounds of sifted white flour exploding in my classroom!"

Outside in the corridor, a look of sheer rapture spread over young Simon Martin's face. Could he be hearing right? One hundred pounds of sifted white flour? Exploding? In the classroom? Oh, bliss and joy! Worth coming back to school. Worth all the miserable hours spent scraping his massive knees under the cramped little desks, being moaned at by teachers, and shriveling with boredom.

One hundred pounds of sifted white flour.

BANG!!!!!

Oh, he could see it now. Drifts of it! Mountains of it! Clouds of it! The room would be knee-deep in flour. It would rain flour. Flour would puff out of the windows, track from the door.

The vision was so beguiling, so white and perfect, so absolutely beautiful, that Simon's ears were temporarily blocked by the ballooning magic force of his imagination, and he completely missed Dr. Devoy's attempt to explain the experiment to his colleague.

"You've got it all *wrong,* Howard. It's the custard cans that explode, not the flour babies. The flour babies are a simple experiment in parent and child relationships. Each boy takes full responsibility for his flour baby for the whole three weeks, keeping a diary to chart his problems and attitudes. It's quite interesting what comes out. It's fascinating what they learn, about themselves and about parenthood. It's a very worthwhile experiment. You wait and see."

Simon caught only the last words, "Wait and see." But he was seeing it already! *BANG!!!!* And then a floury mushroom cloud obliterating the hated prison of the classroom. He rose in spirit with its snow-white glory, and only floated down in time to overhear the last of Mr. Cassidy's desperate attempts to turn down this astonishing and unparalleled blessing.

"Why can't they do something in Mr. Cianelli's workshops?"

A new voice now, raised in anguish.

"Howard! My workshops are buzzing! It's the Science Fair! Why, there's the slopes to set up for the slope friction experiment. And the skeleton house to build for Room 6's electronic burglar alarm system. The base for Harrison's thermistor powered fan hasn't even been begun yet. Nor has the frame for the Lescher twins' electric power station. Even the Maggot Farm needs a few repairs, or we'll have maggots all over."

Simon saw a flash of Mr. Cianelli in the gap, spreading his hands.

"I'm sorry, Howard. It's more than my job's worth to let your pack into the workshops at the moment. Last time I frisked Rick Tullis on the way out, he had four of my screwdrivers stuck down his underpants. Four! And that Tyrone Schumaker of yours only has to *look* at a wood plane for its blade to slip out of true. I'm sorry, Howard. But no."

If Simon hadn't been so outraged with Mr. Cassidy for trying to spurn this gift sent straight from the gods, he might have felt pity at the broken tone of his voice now.

"I won't forget this," Mr. Cassidy was saying. "Next time any of you are in a fix, I'll remember this!"

Prudently, Simon drew his heel back as the voice neared the doorway.

"One hundred and twenty-four pounds of white flour! In my classroom! With that bunch! And not one of you came to my rescue. Not one. I won't forget this. No, I won't forget."

Simon's foot moved sharply away from the door, just as Mr. Cassidy wrenched it open.

"What are you doing here?"

"You *told* me to come here, sir."

"Well, now I'm telling you different. Go away. Go back to the classroom at once."

"Yes, sir."

On principle, Simon stooped, quite unnecessarily, to untie his shoelace and tie it again, in his own time. He wasn't sorry he took the trouble, either, because although the small gesture of defiance earned him a quite alarming glare from Mr. Cassidy, it also kept them both standing there long enough to hear, unmistakably clearly, from inside:

"He's got it wrong again, you know. This time he must have multiplied the one by a seven. It's odd the way his mind works."

Satisfied that honors were now even, Simon shambled off. And Mr. Cassidy shambled after him. He let the boy draw ahead down the long corridor, to give himself time to think. What was the best thing to do? True, he'd made a firm announcement that the very next boy to make any noise at all would have to choose the topic. And Simon had picked the flour babies. But, fair's fair, the lad's Neanderthal door-wrenching habits were purely accidental. He hadn't been trying to make trouble. He just naturally opened doors like a gorilla.

No need to hold firm unnecessarily.

They could just choose again.

Cheered, Mr. Cassidy speeded up. Working things out, he'd fallen quite a way behind. Far enough behind, in fact, to miss Simon Martin's breathless announcement to the waiting class as he burst through the door first.

"Those flour babies! They're going to be the best ever! Terrific! Unbeatable! Better than soap, and maggots, and everything! Best science I've ever *heard!*"

Rolling in twenty seconds later, Mr. Cassidy doused down the noise without even bothering to tune in to its content. He heaved his rump up on the teacher's desk, and began in a conciliatory fashion.

"Well now, Room 8, I'm a reasonable man, and it seems to me on reflection that there's no reason why you should all suffer for the noise Simon Martin makes opening a door. One day, when we have a little more time, we'll explain to him about the principles and use of the door handle. But right now I think we can let bygones be bygones, and go back to discussing the options for the Science Fair."

Simon sucked air in sharply between his teeth. He didn't, on the whole, pay much attention to teachers. But he did recognize their cunning in all its common forms.

"Crafty Old Hopalong!" he muttered bitterly to his neighbor at the next desk, Robin Delaney. "He's just trying to wriggle out of the flour babies because they're the *best*."

Out of sheer habit, Robin passed this intelligence

on. So did his neighbor. So did his. The whisper swept around the room so fast that by the time Mr. Cassidy beamed brightly and asked, "Now, who'd prefer textiles?" they were ranked up and ready with their own form of sabotage.

"Sewing and stuff! Great! You watch out, Delaney! I owe you a good stabbing with the seam ripper, back from last year."

"Bet I can stick fifty pins in my face and keep them there the whole lesson!"

"Bet Tariq can make the sewing machine go so fast it *busts*."

"Can I make a Nazi flag, please, sir?"

"If it's textiles, can we do *stains?*"

"Oh, yes, sir! Yes! I can think of some great stains which wouldn't wash out. *Never*."

Inwardly, Mr. Cassidy shuddered.

"Tell you what," he said brightly. "Let's not bother with textiles. Let's just make it consumer studies instead."

But they were already lying in wait for him on this one.

"Yeah! Yeah!"

"Did consumer studies before. It was really good. Once we had to count how many baked beans there were in eight different kinds of cans. Our team would have won, sir, except for Wayne pigging so many."

"We would have won the value-for-money-in-candies test, too, sir. But Tariq kept spitting them at Phil instead of sucking them steadily."

None of this sort of soft stuff was likely to daunt Mr. Cassidy, Simon could tell. If they were to succeed in their unspoken purpose of making sure everything except flour babies was off the short list, someone had to roll out the big guns.

"You're allowed to go to the mall in consumer studies," he threatened Mr. Cassidy darkly.

And, promptly, the others laid it on as thickly as they could.

"Yeah! Only four of the class came back once. Poor Father Dupinberry took a major fit."

"And Spike nearly got run over. That was a laugh."

"This man jumped out of his car, and as soon as he'd checked that Spike was all right, he bashed him."

"Just for making a dent in his fender, sir. And it wasn't my fault. Luis pushed me."

"Luis was chasing a girl."

Luis gazed around the room proudly.

"I met Francesca, though!"

At the mere mention of Francesca's name, there were animal roars of approval. Promptly, Mr. Cassidy turned his back on the whole pack. He didn't want to have to see the rush of arcane and dubious gestures he knew from experience greeted any female name. In any case, he found the whole idea of sending them trailing around the local shopping mall utterly dispiriting. Why had schools been invented, for heaven's sake? Surely to fill young people's minds

with loftier things than knowing how best to shop for baked beans and dish towels.

No, he'd have nothing to do with this newfangled philistinism.

He picked up the eraser, and with two long, firm strokes, wiped textiles and consumer studies off the board.

"How about home economics?" he suggested.

Cries of contempt rang around.

"Little play houses!"

"Let's pretend!"

"Oh, my! You mustn't use that cloth to polish the forks. You've just used it to wipe the seat of the john!"

"Bring in your washing when it rains, or, guess what! It might get wet!"

"You must be making all this up," Mr. Cassidy accused them sternly. But for the life of him, he couldn't think what else home economics might be about, except stuff that any halfwit could work out for himself in less than a week.

He rubbed home economics off the board.

"You realize," he said, "that only leaves babies and food."

He was convinced that this would settle it. After all, most of the boys in front of him spent half the day industriously filling their faces. You could barely get through a lesson without having to order one or another of them to swallow this, or spit out that, or wrap up the other and put it away until break-time. He should be safely back on home base with food.

But, no.

"We've done nutrition before, sir. It didn't have anything to do with food."

"It's all writing."

"Choosing recipes."

Wayne Driscoll did one of his laborious brain searches, and rather triumphantly came up with a phrase he'd once unwittingly committed to memory.

"Well-balanced meals, sir!"

"What two old codgers with wobbly teeth might have for breakfast."

"It's totally boring."

"No cooking."

"Just looking at charts and stuff."

Mr. Cassidy was mystified. What was the point of worthy citizens forking out to pay for giant gleaming kitchens in schools all over the country if the pupils didn't even use them?

"You must have cooked sometimes," he insisted.

The scowl Tyrone Schumaker turned on him would have frightened stone.

"The only time I got to cook," he said, "I got in a fight with the teacher for scraping it in the garbage after it had been graded."

"I should think so!" said Mr. Cassidy. "What a waste!"

"But I couldn't eat it. It was a meat stew, and I don't eat meat."

"You should have chosen to prepare something different."

Tyrone burned with refreshed outrage at the ancient injustice.

"Why? Nobody said a thing about *eating* it! Nobody even so much as *mentioned* eating it. They went on and on about it being all well balanced, like Wayne says, and having vitamins and such. But nobody ever said a thing about liking it or eating it."

He relapsed into furious muttering.

"And the Old Meanie changed my B to an F. *And* made me rinse out the garbage can . . ."

"What about the rest of you?" interrupted Mr. Cassidy. And with what he thought was real cunning, he offered Simon a chance to shed all the responsibility for having accidentally picked the wrong option in the first place. "How about you, Simon? You'd prefer cooking, wouldn't you?"

Simon gave him a low-grade glower.

"No, I wouldn't."

"Really?" Mr. Cassidy persisted. "Surely a growing lad like you enjoys an occasional extra plate of food."

But Simon had no intention of letting himself be won over. Nor of letting any of the rest of the class be seduced without remembering the grim facts of yesteryear.

"We could have *starved*," he said. "We could have keeled over and *died* before we got around to actual cooking. First we spent weeks and weeks learning how to change ounces into grams, and then we spent weeks and weeks learning how to change them back again, and then we were nagged about eating fi-broids —"

"Fiber, surely."

"Whatever." Simon shrugged off the correction. "But we only got to go in the kitchens twice the whole term."

He couldn't resist adding bitterly:

"And, one of those times, half of us got sent out practically right at the start, just for standing quietly in line."

Mr. Cassidy gave him a look.

"Standing quietly in line? Like in Assembly this morning when I sent you out?"

"Quieter than that," Simon responded virtuously.

"That's right, sir," Robin Delaney backed Simon up. "We were all standing quietly in line."

"Waiting to use the food processor."

"Because we needed to slice our tomatoes."

And, suddenly, Mr. Cassidy could see it. A vision, as if it were in front of him, as if it were this morning. A whole class of them, fooling around in a line, push-ing and shoving and jostling and catcalling one an-other. Half of them holding their tomatoes so care-lessly that watery red drips wept on the gleaming floor tiles. The rest spurting slimy yellow tomato seeds as far as possible up the walls or into one an-other's faces.

"Standing in line," he said. "Just standing quietly in line?"

"That's right," all the ones who had been there assured him.

Mr. Cassidy had put up a good fight. But he was cracking now. Simon couldn't help grinning with pleasure and relief as, watching his teacher intently, he spotted the very moment at which nutrition, as an option, lost its appeal. All Mr. Cassidy could see now, in his mind's eye, was a line of boys waiting for the food processor. Each one prepared to waste almost a whole period standing in line, simply in order to get a turn on that magical whirring and whining machine. Each boy frittering away half an hour of his short life waiting to drop one poor battered lone tomato into the fat round bowel of that precision appliance with all its switches, blades, and speeds. Each boy slowly and impatiently inching forward, ignoring utterly the simple, humble kitchen knife with which, within seconds — no fuss, no mess — he could have chopped or sliced or diced his tomato.

Life was too short for nutrition.

Let it be flour babies. Let chaos reign.

CHAPTER 3

Simon sat across the kitchen table from his flour
baby and gave her a poke.

The flour baby fell over.

"Ha!" Simon scoffed. "Can't even sit up yet!"

He set the flour baby up again and gave her another
poke.

Again, she fell over.

"You're not very good at standing up for yourself,
are you?" Simon taunted, setting her up again.

The flour baby fell over backward this time, off
the table into the dog's basket.

"Damn!"

"You mustn't swear in front of it," Simon's
mother said. "You'll set it a terrible example."

Simon reached down to scoop the flour baby off
Ruggles's cushion, and picked the dog's hairs off her
pretty pink dress.

"Not *it*," he reproved his mother in turn. "*Her*."

She was definitely a her. Definitely. Some of the
flour babies Mr. Cassidy had handed out that morn-

ing could have been one or the other. It wasn't clear. But not the one that landed in Simon's lap.

"Catch, Dopey! Aren't you supposed to be one of the school's athletic heroes? Wake up!"

She was *sweet*. She was dressed in a frilly white bonnet and a pinafore dress, and carefully painted on her burlap were voluptuous round eyes fringed with fluttering lashes.

Robin Delaney, beside him, was jealous instantly.

"How come you get one with eyes? Mine's just plain burlap. Do you want to swap?"

Simon tightened his grip around his flour baby.

"No. She's mine. You paint eyes on your own if you want them."

"And yours has clothes!" He turned to yell at Mr. Cassidy, who was just coming to the end of tossing bags of flour around the room. "Sir! Sir! Simon's doll has a real dress and bonnet and eyes and everything. And mine's got nothing. It's not fair."

"If every parent who had a baby who was a bit lacking sent it back," Mr. Cassidy said, "this classroom would be practically empty. Sit down and be quiet."

He heaved himself up on the desk and started reading the rules of the experiment.

Flour Babies

1. The flour babies must be kept clean and dry at all times. All fraying, staining, and leakage of stuffing will be taken very seriously indeed.

2. Flour babies will be put on the official scales twice a week to check for any weight loss that might indicate casual neglect or maltreatment, or any weight gain that might indicate tampering or damp.

3. No flour baby may be left unattended at any time, night or day. If you *must* be out of sight of your flour baby, even for a short time, a responsible babysitter must be arranged.

4. You must keep a Baby Book, and write in it daily. Each entry should be no shorter than three full sentences, and no longer than five pages.

5. Certain persons (who shall not be named until the experiment is over) shall make it their business to check on the welfare of the flour babies and the keeping of the above rules. These people may be parents, other pupils, teachers, or members of the public.

He looked up.

"That's it."

He'd never seen a class reduced to silence before. An interesting sight. You had to hand it to Dr. Devoy and these scientific types. They had weird powers. Some of them might fumble in and out of the teachers' room, letting their knitted sweaters unravel behind them, and visibly having to comb through their memory banks each time someone asked them if they took sugar in their coffee. But they could work wonders. They could wreak miracles. With their mysterious arts, they could do the unimaginable. They could blow the whole planet to smithereens. They could silence Room 8.

"Well?" he asked, somewhat unnerved. "Any questions?"

Simon picked up his flour baby and lifted up her dress. No underwear, unless you counted the burlap bag. Already she had black smudges on her bottom where he'd sat her on the groove in the double desk along which Robin Delaney's eraser droppings collection had recently overflowed.

"Now look at that," he complained to Robin. "She's already dirty, and it's your fault, Delaney. You're going to have to keep this desk a whole lot cleaner in the future."

Robin stared down at the little heaps of filthy eraser scurf, assiduously kept so he and Simon would always have raw material for flicking pellets. Then he glanced at Simon, trying to work out if he had been joking. Finally, from the quiver of possible responses, he chose the sharpest arrow: ridicule.

"Sir! Sir!" he'd yelled, his fist punching the air as he called for the whole room's attention. "You've got to move me, sir. I can't stay here. It's not safe. Simon Martin's turning into my mother!"

They kept the joke up for the rest of the day. By the time the last bell rang, Simon was absolutely sick of having to prop his flour baby carefully on top of his book bag, then go after whoever it was who'd last called him Old Mrs. Martin, or Mother Sime, and bash his head hard against the wall. By the time he shambled out of the back gate at half past three, his knuckles were burning and his wrist badly grazed. He only stopped himself from wiping the blood off on the flour baby's dress because, through some miracle, he heard the echo of his mother's voice ring out of nowhere in his ears: "Oh, no, Simon! Not blood! It's the *worst!*" He wiped his hand clean down his shirt instead.

And now here was his mother in the flesh, spooning out more free advice.

"You ought to put it in a plastic bag. Keep it clean."

"Is that what you did with me?"

His mother laughed as she dumped his supper down in front of him. Hot dogs and beans.

"I wish I'd had the sense."

She was joking, he supposed. But still, it was a thought. Having him must have made all the difference. He'd come along, a whole other person to be taken into account. Real, too. Not just something like a flour baby that could be shoved in a plastic bag to be kept clean, without ending up on some murder charge. When had she realized how much trouble he was going to be? Some pennies took time to drop. He himself could still remember the day, not that long ago, when he'd first realized he was a person.

He'd been having it out with a turkey. Behind the campground where Simon and his mother went on vacation there was a farm, and one of the larger turkeys had pushed its bad-tempered, gobbling way through the fence and was giving Simon the eye — well, first one eye, then the other — and stopping him from getting to the restrooms.

Simon got even the simplest way he could.

"Thanksgiving!" he jeered. "Here comes dinner!"

The turkey gobbled off. But Simon had to sit on the restroom steps for a moment. He'd suddenly realized that by Thanksgiving the turkey would really be dead on a plate, but (barring the sort of stupid accidents his mother was always warning about), he, Simon, would still be alive.

And somehow that set him off thinking. He pulled the flesh on the back of his hand up into a miniature tent, and then let go. The skin sprang back instantly, keeping him in shape. His shape. It struck Simon for the first time in his life that he was totally unique. In the whole history of the universe, there had never been one of him before. There would never be another.

"Not a very nice place to sit."

Someone was stepping over him to get to the urinals. But Simon, off on another tack, scarcely heard. Once, only a few years ago, Simon *wasn't* — didn't exist at all. And one day, like that turkey, he wouldn't exist again. Ever.

"Can't you find somewhere a bit more *salubrious* to sit?"

The same fellow again, on his way out. Simon paid no attention, his mind on other things. Hadn't he just discovered himself — him — the one and only Simon Martin, alive, and (unlike the turkey) knowing it?

From that day on, Simon had looked at himself with a whole new respect, a far greater interest. The other people at the campground became almost accustomed to seeing the boy from the end tent contorting himself into odd shapes, not like the family near the showerhouse who did yoga, but simply in order to gaze at parts of his body he'd never really looked at properly before: heels, elbows, belly button, inner thighs.

"God knows which parts of himself he stares at in private!"

"Do you suppose the poor boy's *mental?*"

"It's his mother I feel sorry for, really."

"Now stop that, Simon! People will think you've got *lice.*"

Neither the neighbors' whispered comments nor his mother's sharp orders grazed Simon's consciousness. He was busy. Busy probing his huge, lank body with a curiosity, a real wonder, he'd never felt before. All that went through his brain was "This is *me.*" But there was more to it than that, much more, though he could never have explained it, and no one ever asked him.

He had a question for his mother now, though. Picking the last of Ruggles's wiry hairs off the flour baby, he asked:

"What was I like?"

His mother sucked a stray bean off her fingertip.

"When?"

"When I was a baby."

Simon's mother narrowed her eyes at him across the table. Give a boy a doll, she thought, sighing inwardly, and he goes all broody within minutes. What hope is there for girls?

But it was a fair question, and he hadn't asked it for a good long time. Her son deserved an honest answer.

"You were *sweet,*" she said. "Good as gold, and chubby as a muffin, and you had bright button eyes. You were so beautiful that perfect strangers kept stopping the baby carriage in the street to coo at you and tell me how lucky I was to have you. Everybody wanted to blow raspberries on your tummy. No doubt about it, you were the most beautiful baby in the world."

He knew she wouldn't want him to spoil things by saying it, but he couldn't help himself.

"So why did my dad take off so quickly?"

His mother tried her usual tack of making a joke of the whole business.

"Be fair, Simon. He did hang around for six whole weeks!"

But she could tell from the look on his face that the answer wasn't working the way it usually did. So she tried throwing in her Old Witch imitation.

"And deep in the forest are those who say he could see into the future . . ."

But still Simon wouldn't smile.

Mrs. Martin gave up, and took another mouthful of her supper, watching him carefully to try and work out exactly how upset he was.

Simon propped the flour baby up in front of him, and stared at her beautiful round eyes. He felt sour all over suddenly. Suppose his dad *was* able to see the future. Did that make up for Simon not being able to see the past? Anyone who'd ever met their real dad could put it together somehow. Take off some middle-aged spread. Wipe out a few wrinkles. Add a bit of hair. But if you'd never so much as *seen* the man —

"Why aren't there any photographs? I know you didn't have a real formal wedding or anything, but why aren't there any other photos?"

"Simon! There are photos! There are *lots*."

"But not with him. There's hardly a single one of him."

"That's because he was usually the one holding the camera."

"You could have taken at least one good photo of him."

She jammed her teaspoon back in the sugar bowl so hard that sugar flew out and sprayed all over.

"And how was I supposed to know he was going to walk out on me? Women don't always get a week's notice, you know!"

Simon stuck out his tongue, and after a small, insolent pause, began licking the grains of spilled sugar from his wrists. Then he turned his attention to the flour baby.

"Don't lick her, Simon!" And then, instead of adding, "She's been in the dog's basket," his mother warned him: "You might give her germs."

It wasn't a very good joke. But the fact that she'd bothered to try and make one at all made Simon feel better. He realized that, for all she made light of it whenever the business of his father came up, she did understand he had reasons of his own to feel sensitive about the matter. Shoveling the last forkful of beans into his mouth, he asked indistinctly:

"When did you first realize I was a real person?"

He didn't know what answer he was expecting. Maybe "When you were eight" (when he'd refused to go to Hyacinth Spicer's party). Even "As young as four" (when he'd apparently thrown such a tantrum in a shoe store that the manager herself had stepped over and slapped him).

But what she said really surprised him.

"Oh, weeks before you were born! I think we must have been in different time zones. If I was up and about, you were so restful you might not have been there at all. But the moment I laid my head on a pillow, you woke up and started kicking me."

"Soccer practice, see?" he said proudly.

And that reminded him. He glanced at the clock. First practice of the season. Mustn't be late.

"Time to go."

His mother lifted her knife and fork, and slid his plate onto hers.

"Don't let the little lady get muddy," she warned, nodding at the flour baby. "Make sure you put her somewhere safe."

Simon was horrified.

"I can't take it to soccer!"

"Not *it*, Simon. *Her*."

Irritably, he brushed off the tease.

"How can I take her to *soccer?*"

"You have to take her, Simon. It's in those rules you brought home."

Simon cast about desperately for some reason not to take her.

"I can't! It's not just people from our class, you know. There's only me and Wayne from our class on the team. Everyone else will see. They'll laugh us off the field. We'll get crucified!"

"Just keep her out of sight."

"Jeez, Mom!" Had the woman never been in a locker room? Didn't she know your gym bag was not your own? You would be lucky if one time in the whole season you got away without having some joker root through your gear to tug out your underpants and make a great drama of sniffing them and whirling them around his head, or even just borrowing your deodorant or stealing your bus fare.

He'd give a flour baby doll a life expectancy of minutes in a locker room.

Less.

"You'll have to look after it, Mom."

"Me?"

"Just while I'm gone."

She put on her Forget-it-Simon look.

"Forget it, Simon. I'll be out myself until nine. If you think I'm taking your homework with me —"

Simon made his mind up.

"She can just stay here. She'll be all right. It's perfectly safe. I'll shut Ruggles in the living room, so he won't chew her, or anything. She'll be fine."

There was a glint in Simon's mother's eye. Amusement? Interest? Mischief? He couldn't tell.

"And what about Rule 5?"

Rule 5? The snoopers! Simon snatched the list of rules toward him and struggled through Rule 5 again.

> Certain persons (who shall not be named until
> the experiment is over) shall make it their business
> to check on the welfare of the flour babies and
> the keeping of the above rules. These people may
> be parents, other pupils, teachers, or members of
> the public.

Teachers! Old Hopalong must know about soccer practice. What had he said this morning when he tossed the flour baby over? "Aren't you supposed to be one of the school's athletic heroes?" Maybe he'd make it his business to sneak in and rummage through the locker room, looking for his and Wayne's babies.

And "other pupils." Maybe he'd ordered someone

else to check up on both of them. Maybe that Jimmy Holdcroft had been signed on secretly as a nark. He was an oily piece of work. Being a stool pigeon would be right up his street.

And "members of the public." Next door was always twitching her curtains. She was a natural spy. She'd love to gang up with the enemy. All in a day's work for Mrs. Spicer.

No. When it came down to it, no one was safe. You didn't know if you could trust your own mother . . .

His eyes fell on the snooper rule again. "These people may be parents . . ."

Slowly, casually, he turned to look at her. That glint! It was still in her eye!

Oh, surely not. Surely not his own mother. The very idea was ridiculous.

Except —

They'd do *anything,* these parents, if they thought it was good for you, or for your education. In this respect, she had no pride at all. Didn't he know from bitter experience that there were no depths to which she wouldn't sink? Over the years she'd done everything to try and improve his school record. Threats. Bribes. Even punishments. She'd stopped his allowance. She'd grounded him. She'd yelled. She'd begged. Sometimes she'd even cried. (That was the worst.)

Spying on him would be chicken feed. It would be *nothing* to a mother like her. She'd take it in stride.

He couldn't trust her. No, he couldn't trust her.

Sighing, Simon lifted his flour baby off the table and wrapped her carefully in his Tampa Bay Rowdies towel, so just her eyes were peeking out.

"Right," he said. "Off we go. Your first soccer practice. I hope I'm not going to have to remind you how to behave. And I suppose that, on the way, I'm going to have to explain all the rules."

Mrs. Martin moved to the window to watch her son striding down the path, explaining the rules of soccer to a small flour sack with a bonnet and eyes, wrapped up in a Tampa Bay Rowdies bath towel. She wasn't the only one paying attention, she noticed. Next door's drapes were twitching. Mrs. Spicer was watching, too.

And Simon saw. Turning at the gate, he spotted next door's golden brushed-velour drapes shivering in the still air. He broke off his explanation of how an indirect free kick differs from a corner and, leaning closer to his flour baby, whispered in the pointy bit he took to be her ear:

"You can't trust anyone, you know. No. Not around here."

CHAPTER

Boot . . . Boot . . . Boot . . . Boot . . .

Mr. Keller's bellow reached Simon across the length of the soccer field.

"Don't *boot* it, boy! *Tickle* it."

It was Simon's third and last lap. He was pretty fortunate, really. Last year, any member of the team who showed up so late had to do fifty push-ups. Compared with that, dribbling the ball three times around the field was a cinch. Old Keller must be going soft.

Boot . . . Boot . . . Boot . . . Boot . . .

"Are you going cloth-eared, boy? You're not practicing goal kicks! Chase the ball *gently!* Keep it under control. I want to be able to see the elastic holding it to your feet."

It wasn't his fault he'd been late. He blamed Wayne. If Wayne hadn't dragged him off through the empty classrooms, scrabbling through desks to find that bottle of white-out . . .

It was a good laugh, though. Too bad he wasn't

back in the locker room with the rest of them to see Stomper's face when he picked up his can of foot powder and read what it said on the side now: KILLS ATHLETES.

Brilliant.

It was Wayne's idea to paint out the word FOOT. But it was Simon who guessed the comma thing in ATHLETE'S ought to go, too. He wasn't sure. It was just a hunch. But hunches were sometimes right. What about the time he'd been ordered to stand beside Miss Arnott's desk for fooling around in English? She'd been marking some essay of Warren Meyer's called "My Summer Vacation," and muttering to herself under her breath. Then, raising her voice, she'd asked irritably:

"What is this drivel you've written, Warren? '*The Mexicans are all retarded and fiendish*'?"

Warren Meyer had looked baffled. How would he know? He hadn't been on vacation at all. He'd copied the whole thing from Billy Simms, without thinking. But Simon, peering over Miss Arnott's glorious golden summer vacation arm, had taken a stab at it differently.

"I think it says '*The Mexicans are all relaxed and friendly*,' Miss Arnott."

Terrific. Goal! He'd earned a flash of her wonderful smile, and been sent back to his desk in a riot of applause, weighed down by his gleaming halo.

Yes, hunches could work. It was just a pity that, tonight, they'd lost those precious minutes going back to blot out that comma thing. And Wayne hadn't speeded matters up by doing his *Hunchback of Notre Dame* both ways down the corridor. But what took the most time, and landed Simon with his punishment laps, was finding somewhere safe to put the flour babies.

Wayne was for shoving them behind the toilet tank pipes.

"No one will see them here," he'd called down from where he was perched, on a lavatory stall partition. "Throw them up, Sime."

Furtively, Simon unwrapped Wayne's flour baby from the spare shirt in which it was wrapped, and passed it up. Wayne was about to wedge it between the pipes when Simon suddenly asked him:

"Are you sure it's clean?"

Wayne blinked down like an owl caught in a torch's glare.

"Clean?"

"Yes. Are the pipes clean?"

"Grief, Sime!"

But already Simon was stepping on the lavatory seat and hoisting himself up on the partition beside Wayne. He ran his finger along the lower of the two pipes.

"It's filthy! It needs a good wipe."

"Sime! Don't be a plague-spot! We're already late!"

"It'll only take a minute."

Slithering down the partition wall, Simon dived under the nearest sink in search of a cloth.

"Sime . . ."

"Hold on, Wayne. There must be a cloth somewhere around here."

"Sime! Pass my doll thing up! Now!"

"I don't believe this! Ten johns, ten sinks, and no cloth! I mean, I'm not fussy, but wouldn't you think —"

"That's it, Sime!"

Wayne let himself down to the floor, picked up his flour baby, scrambled back up, and shoved it tight between the pipes.

"It'll get *filthy*, Wayne."

Wayne wasn't listening. Rubbing the grime on his fingers off onto his track suit, he made for the door.

"Bye, Sime! Enjoy your push-ups!"

Simon lifted his own flour baby out of his gym bag.

"Come on, sweetheart," he told her. "Let's go outside where it smells less hoofy. We'll find you somewhere nice to sit, in the fresh air."

The place he chose was a bush a few yards behind the one goal still flooded in sunlight. He thrust the flour baby into the rather meager greenery, desperately hoping she would appear to be no more than a bundle of towel to the circle of his teammates already kicking the ball to one another in the warm-up. Mr. Keller was watching him dangerously, arms folded, from the side of the field. But still Simon took his time, wedging the flour baby firmly into the bush. Mr. Keller was the least of his problems. At least now the Snoopers couldn't pick on him. She was there, in sight, and she was clean and safe. Mr. Keller could punish him for being late by giving him fifty push-ups. But if Simon got thrown off the flour baby project, he might miss The Glorious Explosion.

And it was going to be *amazing*. That much he knew. Once or twice since Mr. Cassidy dealt out the flour babies, Simon had suffered moments of doubt. It struck him that he might somehow have misheard the conversation in the teachers' room, or missed the point. And even if he hadn't, one question still remained to be answered. Was the whole business worth it? After all, it wasn't generally Simon's way to stick at a project for the length of a period, let alone for a whole three weeks. Would any — *Could* any explosion Mr. Cassidy had to offer be worth the grind of dragging this flour baby around, keeping her clean, for twenty-one days of his life?

Yes. Yes, it could and would. Hadn't he heard that from the expert himself, Dr. Devoy? Running to join the warm-up, Simon braced himself against the look on Mr. Keller's face by remembering what had happened that very afternoon, in the school corridor. He played it through his brain one more time, like a favorite moment on a video. Mr. Cassidy had been beached up on the radiator outside the classroom door, apparently doing nothing more strenuous than admiring the knot in his laces. It looked the picture of an unofficial break: the teacher idling outside in the corridor, the class causing mayhem within. But anyone who had strolled back late to Miss Arnott's class last year as often as Simon knew the set-up for what it was. Mr. Cassidy wasn't resting. He was listening. In fact, he was about to pounce. What he was doing out there in the corridor was taking a moment to work out to which of the hoodlums inside he would most enjoy awarding a punishment essay.

Simon was accustomed to this old routine. At any moment, Mr. Cassidy would heave his great carcass off the radiator shelf, sidle softly to the door, take a deep breath, and let it out on the other side in such a bellow that poor Miss Arnott, in the next-door room, would all but fall off her chair from fright.

Simon slid back around the corner and waited. From Mr. Cassidy's point of view, he reckoned, the fewer punishment essays to dish out the better. Like Simon, he was not a great reader. If Simon showed himself now, he'd be bound to become Hopalong's prey in an instant. But wait till some other poor victim had been named, and Simon might get a home run through the doorway and back to his desk in all the riot of somebody else's "Who? *Me,* sir? Sir! Why *me?* It isn't *fair!*"

It was worth the risk, anyway.

Simon lounged against the wall, waiting. And that was how he came to see Dr. Devoy and his retinue of willing helpers ("crawlers" to Simon), coming

51 •

around the bend in the corridor. Piled in their arms were all the complicated and unwieldy bits of equipment without which it seemed Dr. Devoy couldn't get through a single forty-minute period in the last weeks before his great Science Fair.

Simon doubled up in a fake coughing fit. Dr. Devoy and his retinue swept past. And Simon stopped coughing just in time to catch Dr. Devoy's remark as he strode past his colleague, still parked on the radiator.

"I see you're starting the semester with a real bang, Howard."

Mr. Cassidy did no more than deal Dr. Devoy one of his poisonous looks, but Simon's doubts were banished and his worries fled away. After all, Dr. Devoy was famous for his extraordinary detonations. His exploding custard cans were the envy of all. If someone with his credentials could admire in advance any big bang of Mr. Cassidy's, then that had to settle it once and for all. The experiment was going to be glorious.

Simon's smile widened into rapture then. And now, as he booted the soccer ball across the circle to Wayne, it was widening again. It was, thought Simon, rather like one of those promises God used to make to those people he kept falling out with in the Old Testament . . . a covenant! They'd done a whole module on them a couple of years back. Rainbows, floods, dead babies — that kind of thing. Well, Dr. Devoy coming down the corridor and saying what he did just as Simon happened to be standing there was a sort of covenant in itself. A private promise between The Explosion and Simon . . .

Mr. Keller materialized beneath his left elbow.

"I see we're in blinders today," he started pleasantly enough as Simon, startled, bungled the next pass. "Not wearing a watch, though, were we?"

No point in *saying* anything, thought Simon. All that would happen is that Mr. Keller would pitch into some fresh complaint about him leaving his underwear trailed over the local greenery. And then the flour baby might catch it.

Simon pawed the ground apologetically with his cleat, and said nothing. Fortunately, just at that moment Stomper Hines and Jerry O'Dell collided with one another, and rolled over and over, inextricably tangled.

Mr. Keller sentenced Simon on the trot.

"Three full laps at the end, please. And *tickling* the ball, not booting it!"

He turned his foghorn voice onto the other two.

"O'Dell! Get your foot out of his face! Get *up*, boy! Go after that ball!"

Simon took off for the safety of the back line while the going was good. He'd escaped push-ups, at least. And the rest of the practice wasn't too bad, what with one short break while Stomper Hines was seriously bawled out for waving through the hedge at his girl-friend, Lucinda, and another a few minutes later when Mr. Keller caught sight of Lucinda for a second time, and held up the next throw-in while he gave her an earful.

So having to stay and dribble the ball three times around the field after everyone else had gone back to the locker room shouldn't have been too much of a pain. Of course he was missing a good laugh: Stomper's look of sheer wonder when he picked up his can of foot powder and, egged on by Wayne, read its vastly inflated claim. But Simon could easily imagine his face. And Wayne would fill him in on details later. So why was he making such a mess of the laps? Why weren't his feet under his control?

Boot . . . Boot . . . Boot . . . Boot . . .

"What *are* you thinking about, boy? Don't hammer it! Treat it gently as a baby!"

Mr. Keller's talk of babies made it worse. Rattled, Simon glanced back over his shoulder at the bush he'd just run past. Was that the right one? Where was the flour baby? Was the little sack of her still propped up safely in the branches, or had the team noticed as they thundered off the field? Maybe Wayne had even squealed on him! Was she still there, all wrapped up and happy as a jaybird, or had they reached in and dug her out? Were they kicking her around the locker room right now, having another good laugh pretending she was a soccer ball?

Stomper would kick her hardest. She'd be *destroyed*.

Distracted, Simon missed the ball entirely.

The bellow came over the field on cue.

"Are you trying to be funny, Simon Martin? You certainly aren't amusing me!"

He nearly missed again. This was unreal. These weren't even difficult kicks. He was only dribbling. And yet he couldn't concentrate at all. How were you supposed to get your feet going in the right directions when your brain was totally cluttered up with horror-show visions of what might be happening to your flour baby? It was a pity Mr. Keller was watching him so closely, or he could spin around, dancing on his toes, and take a good look at the bush. The flour baby was bound to be in there still, all safely bundled up. It was just that he could concentrate better if he was *sure*.

Unwilling to bring the wrath of Mr. Keller down on his head again, Simon didn't turn. He kept his face forward and ran, as one ghastly vision after another swam through his brain. His flour baby floating, face down in one of the scummy sinks, then gradually sinking as the water soaked through her thin burlap! Stomper borrowing a felt pen and, with their unauthorized alterations to his can of foot powder in mind, taking sweet revenge on her face with some artwork: a nose, a gappy smile, two cauliflower ears — worse! And, most disastrous of all, Jimmy Holdcroft drawing back his foot as she lay so vulnerably on the locker room floor, about to demonstrate his vicious and spectacular goal kick.

Simon hurled himself onward. Is this, he asked himself, what people go through every time they

leave a baby sitting in a stroller outside a store? No
wonder they always looked so grim, pushing and
shoving in their hurry to get out again. No wonder
you kept crashing into them, on escalators and in
doorways, determinedly hauling strollers where
strollers obviously couldn't go.

His foot missed the ball again, and it rolled past.

"I'm watching you like a hawk, Simon Martin!
Keep up this performance and you'll be doing push-
ups afterwards!"

Ten yards to the corner. And then, at last, he
would be able to swivel his head and see the bush out
of the corner of his eye. One thing he'd learned, it
was ridiculous trying to practice soccer and watch a
flour baby. No one can do two things efficiently at
the same time. Weren't they always saying that?
"You can't be concentrating on your work if you're
staring out of that window!" And, "No one can talk
and listen simultaneously. If you're talking, you're
not listening." It was one of their regular, all-purpose
naggings.

And his mother was exactly the same. "You can't
do your homework correctly with that radio blaring,
Simon." Or, "Make toast or play with the dog —
one or the other, but not both. That's the fourth slice
of bread that's gone up in smoke!" She knew he
couldn't do two things at once. None of this would
have happened if she'd offered to look after the flour
baby for him. She'd brought him up all by herself,
after all. She must know what it was like. She must

have realized that his soccer practice would turn into a total disaster. Had she forgotten all those evenings she took him with her to the club while she played tennis? They were wretched enough. He still remembered peeling the back of his legs off those horrible plastic bucket seats again and again, in order to drape himself over the balcony, and call down:

"Can we go home now, please?"

Over and over, the same answer floated up from the court.

"Be patient, Simon. We're nearly finished."

He'd sit there for what seemed another fifteen hours, bored out of his skull, and then ask:

"Can I go on ahead?"

"Simon, please! I won't be much longer. This is the last game."

Maybe it was. But as soon as they finished playing it, his mother's partner, Sue, would always act as if Simon's misery and restlessness was just something best ignored, like mosquitoes or rain, and sweep his mother along to the bar for her idea of "just one quick drink." If Simon so much as opened his mouth to complain, he was treated to a lecture along with his Coca-Cola.

"Simon, please! It was a hard game, and I'm thirsty. We'll only be a few minutes. Try and be patient."

He'd sit in a separate booth, sullenly stirring the bubbles out of his drink with his straw while she and Sue chattered away: "Her husband . . ." "My

father . . ." "Their neighbors . . ." "His daughter
. . ." He'd glance around the room for the ninetieth
time. No one his age. No one to stand beside at the
machines. No one to fool around with in the restroom.

He'd hang over the partition between their two
booths.

"Why can't I stay home by myself?"

"Soon, sweetheart. As soon as you're old enough."

"I could have a baby-sitter."

"Simon! It's once a week! For one hour! You know
this is practically the only time I ever get to go out.
Now don't be a pain!"

And he'd been nine or ten. She didn't even have to
watch out for him. He wasn't going to fall out of a
bush and get covered in mud, or be kidnapped and
kicked to pieces in the locker room . . .

Around the last corner! He could see the worst!
Was that really the flour baby, still safely hidden in
the bush? Did the bundle of towel look as bulky as
when he first stuffed it in there? Or had —?

Once more the ball rolled between his feet, un-
checked.

"I'm warning you, Martin! One more duff yard,
and you'll be following this with fifty push-ups!"

It wasn't a job for one person, that was the truth
of it. To look after a flour baby, you needed two. A
substitute. A reserve. Someone with no particular
plans for the evening. He'd heard his mother saying

as much often enough herself when she couldn't find a baby-sitter, or they couldn't afford one. It would have been a whole lot easier if there'd been two of them, that was for sure. Strange, then, to realize he'd never heard her wishing his father back again (unless you counted the time she'd stood at the end of his bed and said rather sourly: "So. Mumps. Pity your father's not here to look after you . . .")

But Simon had missed him. Oh, not personally. It wasn't possible to miss someone whom you'd never known, and whose face was a rather blurry picture. The person Simon missed was someone he made up. Dark and curly-haired, as in the few poor photographs he'd found lying around in drawers. And with a splendid singing voice, as even Grandma still admitted. "A glorious tenor. When he sang out, he made the rafters ring." But it was Simon who threw in the crinkly blue eyes and the strong hands, the grin and the genius at throwing and catching. Long hours of Simon's childhood had been spent working out how his father would come back. One day he'd change his mind. He'd just show up, without any warning, and he and Simon's mother would try again. And this time it would work. He'd want to stay. As Simon sauntered down Revere Street each afternoon on his way back from elementary school, he'd let his thoughts run riot around his father. He would be standing at the gate, his arms outstretched. He'd shout to hurry Simon. And Simon's run would shake the stone sidewalk under his feet, till finally he made it past the last house, and hurled himself into those strong arms.

Ten feet from the corner, Simon would slow his pace, to hold the dream a few moments longer. Then, just as he'd conjured his dad up, he'd snuff him out. Wipe him away, before turning into his own street. It was a trick he'd learned to keep disappointment from rising, like tears, and spoiling the pleasure of getting home.

He'd cried once, though. He hadn't been able to help it. He'd been terribly young — only about six, for heaven's sake. Six-year-olds cried all the time. He had the main part in the Christmas play. (Joseph the car-painter, as he thought at first, till Miss Ness put him straight.) He'd learned his words, and had a scarlet cloak that trailed behind him so importantly that Miss Ness kept saying she ought to take it off him and give it to one of the three kings instead. Each time he wrapped it around himself, he could practically hear trumpets. He waited for the big day in a blaze of excitement.

And then his mother didn't come. He knew she might not, because, when she begged Mrs. Spicer to walk him to school that morning, she was already unsteady on her feet, and coughing horribly. Her eyes were streaming. But through the morning he must have managed to convince himself that she would get there somehow, ill or not, because when the moment came, and Miss Ness pushed him out onto the stage, the first thing he'd done was peer along the rows of faces, desperate to find her.

"I'll be right beside the door if I make it," she'd promised him.

And there was Sue. Funny — he'd never realized before that his mother must have dragged herself downstairs to phone Sue at the last minute. And Sue must have dropped everything — taken a whole afternoon off work and rushed across town — just to be sitting where she'd been told, right beside the door, trying to be someone for him.

It wasn't the same, though. And during the short break between the scenes, Miss Ness, struggling with Hyacinth's huge foil star, forgot for an instant.

"Never mind," she'd said. "Is your dad there?"

The moment the words were out of her mouth, she realized her mistake. But it was too late. He was in floods of tears. She pulled him on her knee and patted him. But it was no good. The tears were rolling and they wouldn't stop. In the end, too many minutes had gone by. The intermission couldn't last forever. So Simon had to let her unpin his glorious scarlet cloak and wrap it around Patrick O'Connor, who had been boasting about knowing everyone's lines from the very first day they had started.

Boot!

He gave the ball a savage kick.

"There you go, Dad," he panted. "That one's for not being there."

He kicked even harder.

"Ever!"

Boot! Boot! Boot!

He could hear Mr. Keller thundering up behind, but he couldn't care.

Boot! Boot!

"That's it, Simon Martin! I've had *enough!*"

BOOT!

Reaching the last stretch, Simon drew back his foot and gave the ball such an almighty kick that it went flying over the roof of the locker rooms.

"That one's for you, Dad," he shouted. "Thanks for *nothing!*"

He realized afterward that he was grateful for the punishment. After all, he was more than fit enough to add on fifty push-ups. The extra effort even dulled the pain. But, best of all, they took a bit of time. Not much more than two or three minutes, even taking them steadily and doing them thoroughly. But long enough — almost exactly long enough — to give the fierce glittering in his eyes time to subside.

CHAPTER 5

"Is this really the kind of thing you had in mind?"

Ambushed on his way out of the teachers' restroom, Dr. Devoy flicked through the sheaf of pages Mr. Cassidy had thrust in his hand.

"Go on," urged Mr. Cassidy. "Read one."

Dr. Devoy glanced, puzzled, at the name scrawled across the grubby sheet of paper on the top.

"Simon Martin? Isn't he one of mine?"

"No, he isn't," snapped Mr. Cassidy. "The one you have is called Martin Simon. You must know the boy — passes exams, reads Baudelaire — that sort of thing. This one is Simon Martin. One of mine. Spends half his time skulking in the lavatories, and the other half shuffling around acting a stick short of the full bundle."

Dr. Devoy couldn't help rebuking his colleague for his unprofessional way of speaking.

"I think you mean, Howard, that he's not yet living up to his full academic potential."

"Just what I said," insisted Mr. Cassidy. "Goes around behaving like a halfwit."

Less than three feet away, behind the door to the boys' lavatories, Simon Martin sank on his heels and buried his head in his hands as Dr. Devoy ploughed through the joint obstacles of crabbed writing and pitiful spelling, to read aloud the first page of his flour baby diary.

DAY 1

I think the whole idea of carrying a flour baby around is completely stupid because she doesn't even cry, or eat anything, or fill any diapers.

Still, mine has been a total drag all day.

I thought my mother was a real meanie for not looking after her for a measly two hours while I played soccer. After all, she's had enough practice looking after people. She's taken care of me for 122,650 hours, if Delaney's calculator works all right. And apparently I was quite noisy, and ate a lot, and made huge messes. Maybe that's why my dad only managed to stick a pathetic 1008 hours. Delaney says that makes him 121.6765 times more of a meanie than my mom, but I'll bet Delaney pressed some of the wrong buttons.

When it came, Dr. Devoy's response was even more of a shock to Simon than it was to Mr. Cassidy.

"But this is splendid, Howard! Absolutely splendid! Look what the boy's learned already. On only the first day he's grasped that, even freed from three of the principal disadvantages of parenthood, the responsibilities are *immense*. He's learned a little about his own early childhood development. And he's even branched out into some quite sophisticated arithmetical calculations, working in tandem with this Delaney."

Behind the door, Simon lifted his head from his hands, and stared at the wall in astonishment. Could he be hearing right? Was this *praise?*

Outside in the hallway, Dr. Devoy glanced again at the laboriously written page.

"Interesting that he already thinks of his sack of flour as female. What do you make of that, Howard?"

But, too excited to wait for Mr. Cassidy's opinion on the matter, he went on to decode Simon's second page.

DAY 2

Today Ruggles got a funny look in his eye, grabbed my flour baby, and gave her a good chew down the bottom of our yard. My mother says I am lucky our dog has such clean slobber and most of it came off.

If I ever have a real baby, I will certainly make sure it gets all its shots against rabies.

I am watching Ruggles very carefully indeed.

65 •

Dr. Devoy waved the page in the air.

"See?" he crowed to Mr. Cassidy. "See, Howard? On the second day he's learning about the staining capacity of canine salivary exudate on woven organic material —"

"Slobber on burlap!"

In his enthusiasm, Dr. Devoy failed to catch Mr. Cassidy's tone of outright scorn.

"Exactly so!" he agreed. "Not only that, but he's already begun to reflect on the vital importance of primary childhood inoculation."

He stabbed the sheet of paper with his forefinger.

"For all we know, Howard, this young man may already have gone to the trouble of looking up the first presenting symptoms of rabies. How else would he know what to watch for in this Ruggles?"

Behind the door, the look on Simon's face was turning from bewilderment to pride. It wasn't often that his work was praised. In fact, now that he came to think about it, he couldn't recall it ever happening before. Maybe he should have stayed in Dr. Devoy's class, where he might have been properly appreciated. It was a shame that interfering earhole Martin Simon had come along and bounced him out of there on the first morning. What did it matter which way around you wrote your name? Martin Simon. Simon Martin. What was the difference, anyway?

Buoyed with fresh confidence, Simon rocked on his heels in happy expectation while Dr. Devoy rustled his way through the loose sheets of paper, searching for the third page of his diary.

DAY 3

Today Hooper got a hold of my flour baby to mess it around, so I called him an animal and stamped on his sandwiches. Then Mr. Cassidy puffed in, saving my flour baby from doom and giving us both a detention.

Not me and the flour baby. Me and Hooper.

Behind the door, Simon lowered his gaze to the tiled floor. For the first time in his life, he regretted not having tried just that little bit harder, done that little bit more. He felt somehow he'd let Dr. Devoy down. And through the door he heard with a twinge of shame the disappointed tones:

"A lot less learned yesterday, admittedly. But never mind, Howard. We will have to content ourselves with hoping the lad makes the very best use of his detention."

His footsteps faded down the corridor, punctuated only by Mr. Cassidy's resonant snort of contempt as he took off in the other direction. Simon crept out. The pile of flour baby reports, he saw, had been dumped on the radiator shelf. Unwilling to go straight along to the detention room and risk his reputation by arriving on time, Simon lounged against the wall, leafing through them.

He found Tyrone's the easiest to read because he'd already heard the story in the locker room, several times, and that gave him a good start.

DAY 3

I took my flour baby on the bus today. It was shoved under my arm, out of the way, till some interfering old trout forced me to sit down and put it on my lap. All the way down Acacia she kept poking it and nattering to it. I thought she was a loony. But when we reached the bus stop at the Eye Center, she got off.

I hope my eyes never go that bad.

Spike Moranis's report was underneath. Simon did have a stab at trying to decipher the first few words. But it turned out to be harder than one of those "*Unscramble-these-letters-to-find-the-names-of-five-vegetables*" quiz books his mother used to waste her time and money buying him before the long bus trip to Grandma's house.

In the end he gave up, and turned to Rick Tullis's effort. He found this one surprisingly easy to read, perhaps because he and Tullis obviously shared a trick or two, both in handwriting and in spelling.

DAY 1

I said I wasn't coming in if we did babies, and if Mr. Henderson hadn't spotted me outside of the mall I wouldn't be here today.

I definitely won't be here tomorrow. Or the next day. Or —

Suddenly recalling that the minimum number of sentences for the daily entry was three, Rick Tullis had broken off promptly at this point, considering duty done.

Simon ran his eyes a second time over Tullis's brief and sullen report. Perhaps he was still warmed by Dr. Devoy's generous praise. Perhaps the glimpse of insight came spontaneously. But, staring at Rick Tullis's niggardly and mean-spirited scribblings, Simon saw for the first time why teachers showed such scorn for those who did as little as possible. He understood why one class after another was shot through with their howls of exasperation and anguish.

"Believe me, George O'Rourke, it's not *me* who's the poorer for your not bothering to do your homework. It's *you*."

"To me, Tullis, this blank page signifies just one more piece of paper I don't have to take home and mark. To you, on the other hand, it signifies yet another blank patch in your brain."

"I know I didn't specifically say *you* had to do it, Luis. I'm not in the habit of saying 'Everyone has to do the work, and that also goes for Luis Pereira.' "

Suddenly it all *meant* something to Simon. He was struck by the sheer grit of teachers. Their stout hearts. Their unflagging fixity of purpose. Determinedly they soldiered on, term after term, trying to

make their pupils give of their very best. And with what results? With what thanks? Simon was appalled to think how often he (and so many others) had insulted these dedicated saints in human form by handing in such shoddy work. How *could* he have been so ungrateful? How *could* he?

There and then, Simon vowed to make amends. He would begin by fulfilling Dr. Devoy's fond hope that he'd make the best use of his time in the detention room. Resolutely, he shoveled the pile of flour baby reports back on the radiator shelf, scooped up his book bag and strode off down the corridor, not even stopping to draw one or two tiny cartoon figures on this week's wall display, as usual.

Hearing the door shudder horribly on its hinges, Miss Arnott looked up. When she saw it was Simon Martin, she couldn't help sighing. She'd had him in detention often enough before, and, unacquainted with his change of heart, all that went through her mind was that his arrival presaged, as usual, a farewell to quiet marking, an end to peace.

She leaned back in her chair and waited for the performance. What would it be for starters? A swipe at Hooper with the book bag, of course, just to remind him of his joint role in whatever villainy it was that had landed them there in the first place.

Then to warm up, perhaps, the drama of the pencil. Its noisy and argumentative borrowing, followed, in natural order, by its sharpening, its dropping with a clatter, its ostentatious chasing across the

floor and its resharpening, then the flicking of its broken point at one of the window panes. Hearing the *ping*, Miss Arnott would be expected to raise her head in time to watch the pencil finally being used — as a drumstick for the tattoo on the desk top.

Unless, today, he chose to stage one of her favorite entertainments: the Bloodied Tongue. Last time she supervised Simon Martin, he had gone to some trouble and effort to suck enough ink out of his pen cartridge to stain his tongue bright red. He'd let this gory-looking monstrosity hang out of his mouth for the whole of the rest of the detention, rendering her incapable of eating her sandwich but amusing her mightily. Miss Arnott secretly hoped she might be treated to the Bloodied Tongue again today.

Though what she liked most of all was his Rip Van Winkle. She found that tremendously soothing. Simon would sprawl over the desk, give a few gargantuan yawns, and then appear to fall into a sleep so deep no one could wake him for a hundred years. From time to time (whenever he feared that she'd forgotten him), he'd snore: a gentle faraway ripple that swelled ever richer and deeper, until each lungful of air that he released was reverberant enough to set the window frames rattling. Just as she began to fear for the structure of the building, he'd let out a giant snort and pretend that he'd woken himself. He'd stare around blankly, smacking his lips like an old man. And then he'd settle back down on the desk, and replay the whole performance from start to finish.

Yes. Rip Van Winkle was her favorite. The act she didn't like was Gibbering Idiot. She'd seen it too often and was bored with it. He'd sit at his desk, making grotesque faces. Every now and again he'd erupt into fits of maniacal laughter or frantic bursts of muttering. Sometimes he drooled. She hoped it wasn't going to be the Gibbering Idiot. But, just in case, Miss Arnott reached in her bag, to check that she still had her aspirin.

And her hand froze. Before her eyes — was she dreaming? was this really happening? — young Simon Martin crossed the room, ignoring Hooper totally. He drew out the chair behind the desk farthest from the three other malefactors she was watching, pulled his flour baby, a pad of paper, and a pen from his book bag, and, without making any fuss, propped the flour baby up on the desk top, patted her head affectionately once or twice, then settled straight down to work.

Miss Arnott blinked.

"Simon?" she whispered. "Simon, are you all right?"

He looked up.

"Excuse me?"

It sounded almost like a mild rebuke, as if she'd interrupted him in an important train of thought.

"I was just wondering if you were all right."

He stared at her.

"Yes. I'm all right. Why?"

She shook her head.

"No reason."

And for the life of her, she couldn't think of any. Except that it wasn't *normal*. Well, it was normal, of course. But that was exactly what was wrong. With Simon Martin, acting normal wasn't normal.

Maybe the lad was sick — feverish, perhaps. Or maybe he was in shock. It's possible that he'd just heard his mother had been knocked down by a truck, or electrocuted changing a plug, or drowned in a creek, or —

Miss Arnott tried to pull herself together and dismiss the lurid flow of her imagination. Surely a pupil should be able to sit down and quietly busy himself with a bit of written work without one of his teachers presuming he needed an ambulance, or his mother was already inside one!

She tried to go back to her marking. But it was impossible. She couldn't concentrate at all. She kept having to raise her eyes from the books, and check on Simon Martin. What was he writing so industriously? He seemed to be covering whole sheets of paper. She'd taught him English for two whole years, and in all that time she never once saw him cover half a page in less than a double period. Who or what could have inspired the boy to scribble away so busily today?

Miss Arnott had to know. Slipping from the desk, she crept around the room on her rubber soles, till she was directly behind him. She leaned forward a little, so she could see over his shoulder. And with two years of decoding the work of Spike Moranis in her professional armory, Miss Arnott no longer had any problem at all deciphering Simon's crabbed writing and his unique spelling forms.

DAY 4

Until I was forced to lug this stupid flour baby around with me everywhere I go, I never thought about my dad having to take care of me. When I asked Mom, she said he wasn't too bad at it really. He never dropped me on my head, or left me floating face down in the tub while he went off for a towel, or anything like that.

It's just that he didn't stay.

I've asked why he left before. Mom and Grandma always say it didn't have anything to do with me, it wasn't my fault, and it was bound to have happened anyway. But last night I asked Mom how he left, and when she tried to wriggle out of answering, as usual, I wouldn't let her.

Simon broke off. He wasn't sure how to describe what happened next. His mother had rolled up her eyes, the way she always did when she was getting fed up with a conversation.

"How many times do I have to say it, Simon? I don't *know* why he left."

"But I'm not asking *why*. I'm asking *how*."

"How?"

"Yes. How? How did he go? What did he *say*? What did *you* say? Was there a giant fight? Was Grandma there?"

He leaned across the table.

"I'm not asking you to tell me what was inside his *brain*. I'm asking something different."

She was close to defeat. He knew it, and pressed his advantage home.

"I have a right to know."

She reached over the table and patted his hand.

"I know, I know."

But she said nothing more. So Simon pushed on.

"You've finished with *him,* right? And he's definitely finished with *us.* He's disappeared, never sent any money, and never even written. I bet, after all this time, even a private detective couldn't find him."

He pulled his fingers out from under her hand.

"But *I'm* not quite finished with *him.* See? There are some things I think about. Things I want to know. And this is one of them."

He stared down at his battered knuckles, close to tears.

"Please, Mom. Tell me about the day he left."

And so she told him — told him everything — right down to what his father had for breakfast that morning, and what he was wearing, and even the withering things he said about the people in the next-door apartment when their dog started barking at the mailman as usual. She told him all the things his father did that morning, and what they had for lunch.

She even remembered the joke he made to Sue when she came around, about needing her regular Saturday afternoon fix of cuddling the baby.

"Me."

"You."

She spread her hands, like someone trying to convince a policeman of her innocence.

"Honestly, Simon," she said. "Nothing was different. There wasn't anything about the day to make it special. So far as anyone could make out afterwards, your dad wasn't in a mood, or feeling jealous or left out, or anything. In fact, when he disappeared, everyone thought that something terrible must have happened — a road accident or something. It was only afterwards we figured out that sometime in the afternoon he must have packed the large blue bag and lowered it out of one of the back windows on a rope. When he strolled out of the gate, he wasn't carrying a thing. He had his hands in his pockets and he was whistling. We thought he was going to buy beer, or a chocolate bar or something. But he must have walked around to the back of the building, picked up his bag, and gone to the bus station — timing it perfectly for the last bus to Chicago."

She gave a rueful smile.

"As soon as she heard that, of course, your Grandma went *wild*."

And now Simon couldn't help smiling as well. He could imagine it. Grandma on the phone the day her son-in-law did a major flit.

"Volcanic!"

His mother took the opportunity to rise from the table. Clearly she was hoping the conversation was over.

Simon called her attention back, just for a moment.

"What was he whistling?"

She turned and stared.

He asked again.

"What was he whistling? When he strolled out of the gate with his hands in his pockets, what tune was he whistling?"

She shook her head.

"Oh, Simon! How should I remember that?"

He didn't push his luck saying so, but for the life of him he couldn't see why it was any more strange than remembering whether a man had cornflakes or granola the day he walked out of the gate and down the street and out of your life forever. Surely the song he was whistling was far more important. It might, after all, be a clue to what he was thinking. And what would someone only a very few years older than Simon himself have in his mind as he walked out to begin his life all over again, somewhere different. What would he be whistling? "Faraway Roamer"? "Long and Lonesome Road"? "Goin' to the City and Ain't Never Comin' Back"?

And now, in the stuffy detention room, the tunes he'd thought of came back, one by one, and idled through his mind as his pen tracked over the paper, steadily setting down in his flour baby diary everything his mother had told him the night before. When little snatches of song broke through his clenched teeth in a soft whistling, Miss Arnott didn't bother to hush him. He wasn't trying to disturb the others, after all. He didn't even seem to realize he was doing it. And while he was so absorbed, she could keep making her quiet circuits of the room, and come up behind to peep over his shoulder and read the last few sentences he'd written.

> And what was strangest of all the things
> Mom said was that my father wasn't even in
> a mood or feeling mean that day. Somehow
> that makes it seem as if he wasn't so much
> leaving us as moving on to whatever it was
> he wanted next. And I've realized something
> else. I've realized that, if I hadn't been there,
> already born, my dad would by now be just
> one of those old boyfriends that Mom's
> forgotten completely. If they hadn't had me
> between them, she probably wouldn't even
> get his name right by now, let alone
> remember what he looked like and what
> he ate for breakfast.
> I just wish I knew what he was whistl—

The bell rang.

Miss Arnott jumped back so when they all swiveled in their seats to look at her hopefully, Simon wouldn't realize she'd been reading his work.

"Is that it?"

"Yes. Off you go."

He wasn't as quick as usual at stuffing his things in his bag, and making for the door. Miss Arnott took the chance to speak to him.

"Simon —"

He turned.

She didn't know quite how to put it without insulting him. In the end, she just said companionably:

"You wrote an awful lot today."

He shrugged.

She tried again.

"Sometimes people just take time to get started with schoolwork. Late bloomers, we call them. They fool around for years, not really seeing the point of any of it. And then one day light dawns, and they actually begin to enjoy it."

She waited.

Simon said nothing.

She knew she might as well drop it. But out of sheer, burning curiosity, she couldn't help trying one last time.

"Do you think that might be what's happened to you today?"

Simon inspected his huge feet. He didn't actually regret putting his energy into his work for the whole period. But most of the early enthusiasm, and all of the guilt, had drained away now. He felt like an empty pen cartridge, used and spent. Just for a moment he did consider the idea of trying to stay a new person, a born-again Simon, religiously doing his homework and handing it in on time, spending his lunch hours in the library, discussing study projects in depth with his teachers. After all, the last forty minutes hadn't been too bad. His hand was aching, yes. And there was a red patch on the side of his finger where he'd been gripping the pen (though that was nothing compared with the battering he took for granted in ten minutes of soccer). No, what Simon didn't like — stronger than that, what he *hated* — about the last forty minutes was that they'd gone. Gone for ever. Snap! Just like that! And he'd been concentrating so hard, he hadn't even noticed them going. For forty minutes he'd been behaving like one of those earholes in all the other classes — the kind who might look up from the last page of the book they were reading, and be astonished that it had gone dark.

No. Your whole life could go down the drain that way if you didn't keep a look-out. You had to be very much on your guard.

Miss Arnott was still gazing at him hopefully. And Simon had always been very fond of Miss Arnott. He didn't want to be the one to crush her starry-eyed teacher's dream.

Shuffling his feet, he made a real effort to be diplomatic.

"Possibly," he said. And then again, with a little more firmness: "Possibly."

And to keep her from harrying him further, he made for the door as quickly as possible.

Outside in the corridor, Simon found himself pinned against the wall by what he at first took to be a miniature armored car.

Over the top of it, Tyrone was grinning like a fool.

"So what's *this?*" Simon demanded.

Tyrone pulled back a few inches so Simon could free himself and take a better look.

"Isn't it obvious? It's an old baby carriage."

"So why's it got eight wheels?"

Tyrone rolled his eyes.

"Because it's actually two baby carriages lashed together with some wire Tullis pinched for me, that's why."

"But what's it for?"

"Flour babies." Tyrone's eyes shone. "Look, Sime. How many flour babies do you reckon you could shove in this front one without any falling out?"

Simon tugged his flour baby out of his book bag, and sat her at one end, like a queen.

"About ten," he said, after a moment's reflection. "They'd be a bit squashed, but they wouldn't fall out."

"Exactly!" crowed Tyrone. "Ten in this one at the front and nine in this one at the back. All nineteen flour babies fit in the two tied together."

"So?"

Tyrone was getting impatient.

"Don't be such a dim bulb, Sime! It's a little traveling nursery. Day care on wheels!"

"Suffocation on wheels, more likely," said Simon, unconvinced.

Tyrone started pushing. Rigidly lashed together as they were, the two baby carriages were impossible to maneuver around the corner, and Tyrone was reduced to doing a seven-point-turn under Simon's strident but unsystematic instruction.

"But that's the whole point," he insisted, as the two of them finally took off at last down the straight. "The more flour babies I can cram in, the more money I make."

Simon was mystified.

"Money?"

Tyrone turned to stare.

"This isn't going to be *charity* day care," he told Simon sternly. "If I'm taking responsibility, I'm taking money. That's business."

Simon said disparagingly:

"Come off it, Tyrone. No one will sign up for this. No one."

"Oh yes, they will," Tyrone informed him cheerily. "I've got ten names down already, and three more going home tonight to sift through their money bags and see if they can afford —"

Whoooomph!

He'd run into Dr. Devoy, who was rounding the next turn in the corridor at such a speed he couldn't stop in time. Simon expected the worst. A thundering lecture. Another detention or a punishment essay. But Dr. Devoy, when he caught his wind, simply prowled around the strange eight-wheeled vehicle, eyeing its visible features and weighing up its attributes.

"Extraordinary!"

He spun around to address the little crowd of acolytes trailing behind him with their arms full of laboratory equipment.

"Extraordinary! Most fortuitous! Here we were only this morning discussing articulation in vehicles, and here in the corridor is a perfect example of exactly what I was trying to explain. Note that, with a rigid rectangular structure of these proportions and —"

Here, he broke off to peer briefly under the carriages.

"Eight wheels —"

Distracted, he stopped again.

"What is this?" he asked, pointing. "Is this thirty amp fuse wire? I certainly hope it didn't come from any of Mr. Cianelli's workshops!"

Then, without even waiting for an answer, he ushered his little group on, still lecturing them mightily about such mysteries as angles of approach, and separate speeds and velocities.

Simon and Tyrone lounged against the wall and watched them walk away. Tyrone was relieved that Tullis's theft of ten yards of fuse wire had not fully registered with Dr. Devoy, and Simon was reassured that his decision not to become one of the earholes had been exactly the right one. Just for the moment, he felt safe again.

They watched in silence for a few more seconds.

Then Tyrone nudged Simon as the last of Dr. Devoy's retinue disappeared around the bend in the corridor.

"Sad lives . . ." he said, shaking his head.

Simon echoed,

"Sad lives . . ."

Forcibly they shook themselves out of the mournful mood into which what little they understood of the impromptu lesson on articulation had unaccountably thrown them.

Together they pushed the baby carriages off down the corridor to find somewhere with a steep slope, and cheer themselves up with a good laugh.

CHAPTER 6

On Day 11, Robin Delaney lost his temper and kicked his flour baby in the creek. It sank almost at once. Three days before, at the twice weekly weigh-in, things had been going well enough. His flour baby hadn't lost any weight from ill-treatment. Nor had it gained any from added damp. But on the way home from school on the eleventh day, something in Robin snapped, and the result was a few rising bubbles, and a line of curious faces peering into the filthy black water of the creek.

"Death-blow!"

"Seriously sunk, Delaney!"

"You *and* the baby . . ."

"Why did you *do* that?"

But Robin seemed reluctant to explain.

"I just couldn't help it, you see?"

"No," Simon said, pulling his own flour baby's bonnet straight. "I don't see. I don't see at all."

Robin scowled at him horribly.

"Well, maybe your flour baby is a whole lot easier to look after than mine."

"Oh, sure!" scoffed Simon, though secretly he did think that it might be true. His own flour baby had a way of watching with those big round eyes that made her easy to look after. He often found himself chatting to her companionably. "Comfy?" he'd ask, as he propped her on top of the rest of the stuff in his book bag. "Happy?" as he lifted her to the top of the dresser (the only place Ruggles couldn't get at her). Using his flour baby to join in a glorious explosion was going to be difficult enough. But at the very least it would be something extraordinary, something quite awesome. He couldn't imagine just booting her into the creek.

"What made you *do* it?" he asked again.

If it had been only Simon who was curious, Robin would have ignored the question. After all, everyone in the whole school knew by now that Simon Martin had gone moon-eyed about his bag of flour. But the other three were watching him as well. Warren Meyer had even slid off his bike. Everyone was standing waiting for his answer. They were, he thought, like a pack of jackals closing in on some poor wounded fawn.

"I don't *know* why I did it," he snapped. "I just lost my temper, all right? I just got sick of the stupid thing staring at me day after day."

"Yours didn't stare," Simon couldn't help pointing out. "Yours didn't have any eyes."

Robin turned on him.

"Oh, go walk the plank, Sime! It's all right for you. You don't mind going around acting like a major nerd. Nobody's going to laugh at you, are they? Nobody's going to tease someone the size of a gorilla for strolling around and tickling a six-pound bag of flour under the chin, and singing it lullabies —"

"Now look here, Delaney —"

But Robin was too annoyed to stop.

"It's all right for you, you great big-fisted ape. Nobody tangles with you. But what about the rest of us?"

"Yeah!"

"Too true!"

"Delaney's right."

Simon spun around to face the gang of traitors behind him.

"You're not taking *his* side?"

But it seemed they were.

Wayne Driscoll was the first to testify.

"Robin's right. I'm sick of mine, too. I'm sick of carrying it around everywhere I go, and trying to keep it dry and clean. I'm sick of the way it gets dirtier and dirtier without me even *looking* at it! I'm sick of putting it down somewhere perfectly all right for half an hour, and then, when I pick it up again, it's practically gone *black*. I tell you, I'm just about ready to boot mine in the creek as well."

Simon tried to be reasonable.

"Why don't you put it into Tyrone's day care? He keeps them safe and clean."

Wayne had the answer ready.

"I haven't got any *money*."

"You could just *owe* the money to Tyrone."

This time, Wayne couldn't help laughing in his face.

"Do me a favor, Sime! If you weren't so busy cuddling your new doll all day, you'd know that Tyrone's already hired Henry and Billy to punch the money out of anyone who falls behind with their day care payments. Why do you think George is walking home with us today? He's had his bus fare robbed by Tyrone's hard nuggets."

Bitterly, he tilted his head to one side and did a creditable imitation of Tyrone saying, "Very sorry, folks. That's business!"

But George was already pushing him aside in his eagerness to expand on his complaints himself.

"That's right. I'm sick of walking home. I'm sick of handing over all my money to Tyrone, just to have a few measly hours off looking after this stupid thing every day. And I'm sick of getting no sympathy. Last night I was explaining how unfair it all was to my mother, and she just laughed. In fact, she said she wished Tyrone had been running his day care when me and my brother were babies, because she'd happily have paid double the price he charges to get rid of us for a few hours. She says this flour bag is *nothing* to the trouble and bother of a real baby. She says, when it comes to looking after things, I don't even know I'm *born*."

His face went dark.

"I don't get hardly any money anyway. I've already had to borrow from next week's allowance to pay Tyrone back for last week. I can't go on like this. By the time I give back the flour baby, I shall be months in debt. Months! I'm for kicking the thing in the creek now."

Before Simon could argue, Warren Meyer had chimed in.

"Me, too! I'm fed up with mine. I'm fed up with having to tie the stupid thing safely on the back of my bike, and then go to all the extra trouble of wrapping it in a plastic bag in case some car wheel goes through a puddle and soaks it. I'm fed up with my mom and dad reminding me to take it upstairs with me every night, and bring it down again in the morning. I'm fed up with having to make sure it's never left alone in the same room as our cat. I'm ready to kick mine in the creek along with everyone else's."

And, to prove it, he started ripping the plastic bag containing his flour baby off the back of his bike.

Simon was about to snatch it safely away when Wayne Driscoll stepped in front, holding his own flour baby ready for a drop-kick.

"Let's have a competition!" he shouted. "See who can boot his flour baby farthest into the creek!"

"See whose sinks quickest!"

"See whose makes the most bubbles!"

Simon moved closer to the creek, spreading his arms wide, to stop them.

"*No!*"

For a moment, they turned their attention back on him.

"Don't be such a pathogen, Sime!"

"Wimpo!"

"I tell you, this flour baby business is turning you into a real *stain*."

Simon stood his ground between the four of them and the slippery edge of the creek.

"Listen," he begged. "I know you hate them. I know you all think they're stupid and not real science and not worth bothering about, and you'd rather get pulped by Old Hopalong for losing them than trail them around one more day."

He spread his hands.

"But it's going to be worth it," he assured them. "It is! It is! If you can just hold on —"

His eyes shone with the vision that had sustained him through eleven days.

"It's the explosion, you see," he explained. "It's going to be brilliant. Amazing! Like one of those things in the Bible — you know — blood rivers and plagues of frogs and locusts and first-borns, and stuff like that. I promise you, it's going to be one hundred pounds of sifted white flour exploding all over our classroom!"

"Delaney's didn't explode when he booted it," George pointed out sourly. "Delaney's just *sank*."

Fired with the iron conviction of the religious fanatic, Simon had no trouble at all coming up with a reason to dismiss this rather inconvenient observation.

"Delaney couldn't have booted it hard enough."

Here was a challenge indeed. The little gang of them eyed one another, weakening.

Wayne was the first to crack. After all, he'd poured scorn on Robin Delaney often enough in games over the last three years. And facts were facts. Robin could barely kick a ball out of a paper bag.

And it was true that, after eleven miserable days spent shackled to a flour baby, one brief booting of the thing into the creek did not match the glorious vision Simon kept holding out to them. Wayne wouldn't put money on anyone else's flour baby exploding over the water, anyway. Warren's goal kick was worse than Delaney's. And George's was no better. Their sacks of flour would probably sink, just like Robin's, without a trace. His own would explode, all right. No doubt about that. He wasn't on the soccer team for nothing. But even then the flour would simply blow away over the water. There wouldn't be a good and lasting mess.

No. Whichever way you looked at it, one hefty kick over the creek would not make up for eleven ruined days.

"All right," said Wayne. "You win. We'll wait."

But there was still an unbeliever in their midst.

"Why?" George O'Rourke suddenly demanded.

"Why should we wait? Just because Sime here keeps going on and on about his wonderful explosion? You're crazy if you believe him. He must be wrong. Mr. Cassidy has taught in that classroom for *four hundred years*. He isn't going to let anyone kick a hundred pounds of flour around in there. He'd have to be out of his mind. No. It'll never happen. Sime must have got it all wrong."

Simon's voice rang with honest conviction.

"It's what he *said*," he insisted. "I *heard* him. Don't forget I was eavesdropping right outside the teachers' room door! 'Over a hundred pounds of sifted white flour exploding in my classroom.' That's what he *said*. His exact *words*."

Now Wayne was torn between sense and desire.

"I don't know," he said, scuffing the side of his shoe against a clump of grass on the creek edge. "It sounds pretty unlikely. But maybe Sime is right. After all —" His voice rose as the rigor of his thinking was suddenly overwhelmed by the strength of his feelings. "After all, why else would we be forced to look after these floppy, useless, pathetic things for three whole weeks, with people snooping to make sure we do it right, if not to get us all so boiling mad, we kick the stupid things to bits?"

He glowered around, demanding an answer.

"We were *told* why," George O'Rourke reminded him. "It's to learn about ourselves, and how we feel about the job of being a parent. That was the point."

"Then it didn't matter that I booted mine in the

creek," Robin said cheerfully, "because I didn't learn anything from it. Not one single tiny thing. I dragged that stupid bag of flour around for eleven whole days, and all I learned is that I never, *ever* want a baby in my whole life unless someone else offers to look after it at least half the day, and there's a free day care center next door!"

Everyone fell silent.

"It seems to me," said Wayne, "that if people had the faintest idea what a bother babies are, no one would ever have one."

"And," added Robin, "if they happened to end up with one by accident, anyone with any sense would run away."

He looked to Simon for agreement. But Simon turned his back.

Then Robin realized.

With a guilty glance at the others, he reached out and laid his hand on Simon's shoulder.

Instantly, Simon shook it off, and marched back along the creek the way they had come.

"What's up with him?" George O'Rourke asked, mystified.

"Shut up, you great hiccup," whispered Robin. And he couldn't help adding importantly: "Didn't you know Sime's dad only lasted six weeks of taking care of him?"

"No," George said. "I didn't know that."

He stared after Simon.

"Not very long to have a dad, is it?" he said.

Robin said portentously:

"It is exactly one thousand and eight hours."

Everyone looked at Robin with a new respect. Then, one by one, they turned to watch in sympathy as Simon drew farther and farther away from them along the creek. It was perfectly clear that he didn't want their company any longer.

Warren got back on his bike.

"I'm going home now."

George nudged Wayne. "Come on. Let's go." He pulled Robin along with them. "You too, Robin. No point in staying here. He won't turn around and come back until we've all gone."

And he was right. A minute or so after they disappeared between the trees on the bend, Simon glanced around to check that the path was clear, and only then did he turn back again. Simon felt terrible. Unfit for company. Best left alone.

Six weeks! Six whole weeks! *Surely,* he thought, as he kicked moodily at stones along the path, six weeks was long enough! What could have been *wrong* with him as a baby? What sort of little blot could he have been, that after six whole weeks his father hadn't even thought him worth staying around for, worth bringing up? Simon had only had his flour baby eleven days, and already, just as he couldn't imagine himself simply booting her into the creek out of temper, so he couldn't think how his own father could just have walked out, whistling, one fine day. After all, Simon was *real*.

So what had been wrong with him? Simon had seen other babies. Only that morning, on the way to school, he'd practically bumped into one. It was stuffed into one of those backpacks, and its mother was standing at the curb on the corner, waiting for the light to go green. Eleven days before, Simon could have strolled past whole swarms of babies, and not even noticed them. Now he saw every one.

It was wearing a bonnet studded with woolen knobs, with a ribbon bow under its chin. Both the baby and the bonnet looked very *clean*, Simon thought. Cheeks pink and gleaming. Wool white as snow. He wondered how the parents managed it. For all his own studious efforts to protect her, his own flour baby seemed to be getting grubbier by the day.

As if sensing his rather envious stare, the baby turned in the backpack to look at Simon. Its ribbon chin strap slipped across its mouth, and Simon stretched out a finger, thinking to push it back.

The baby saw the finger coming. Instantly its bland pudding face was transfigured with a smile. To Simon it looked as if some mighty lightbulb had just been switched on in the baby's head. The effect was magical. The little face shone.

Simon grinned at the baby. What a cinch! To judge by the way it was beaming, you'd think Simon had just performed some absolutely unbelievable trick, some astonishing feat, like doing a triple somersault with sparklers sticking out of his ears, and not just stuck out a grubby finger.

He hooked the ribbon back under the baby's chin. It didn't flinch. Clearly it was so amazed and thrilled by the mere sight of the finger coming close that it didn't even realize the point was to tug the bonnet straight.

Drunk with power, Simon waggled the finger.

Instantly the baby was reduced to paroxysms of mirth. It squirmed energetically in its backpack.

Its mother turned around.

"Sorry," said Simon, and the light turned green.

All the way over the road, Simon stayed a step behind the baby, waggling his finger just above its head. The baby kicked and crowed. Simon felt quite a pang when he had to peel away on the other side. He couldn't remember ever delighting anyone so much, so easily. How old was that baby? He had no idea. He knew almost nothing about them. He did suppose that if one of those tiny, purplish newborn ones he'd seen on documentaries was put beside one of the hulking great pink ones you saw outside stores, he'd be able to tell the difference. But that was about it. Maybe, thought Simon, his dad was a duffer about babies too. Maybe, when he looked down at Simon gurgling blankly in his crib, he hadn't realized that within weeks — or was it months? — he'd turn into something like that baby at the traffic lights, who could make you feel like a million dollars just for being able to waggle a finger.

That was the thing about babies, Simon decided. They were different from everything else. They were

special. All of a sudden it was clear to him why everyone in the whole world was forever standing in line
to blow raspberries on their tummies. Even if you
were a complete hiccup, leading a totally sad life, a
baby thought you were a real star, the best thing since
sliced bread, and worth falling out of a backpack to
get one last backward look at. Small wonder everyone went around saying "Ooh!" and "Aah!" and
cooing about how much they adored them. Before,
Simon had always assumed that this was simply a
kind of act, to try and cheer up the new parents. It
never occurred to him for a moment that it was sincere. But now he saw people meant it. They were
saying what they thought. Babies were wonderful.
And it was no more than the truth. Face facts —
you'd never get something that good down at the
mall.

And what was so good about them was that they
weren't really people — not yet, anyway. And so you
could treat them differently. It was easier to like
them. In fact, they were a little like pets, the way you
could feed and clean and tidy up after them day after
day, and even if you got bored and irritated, you
didn't feel they should be pulling their weight more.
No one in his right mind would get all huffy because
a baby wasn't doing as much for him as he was doing
for the baby.

But people were a whole knottier prospect, with
one side or another always feeling put upon, or taken
for granted. Why, even Stomper had been given the

final flick by Lucinda three days ago, for much the same sort of problem. "I'm finished with you!" she'd yelled at him. "I'm sick of living on a one-way street! I cheer you on in all your soccer matches. I even watch you practice. And what happens when I ask you to come and root for me in my tennis final? You say you don't have time!" And now, each time Stomper phoned her after school to beg her to come out and talk, that's all she'd say to him: "I don't have time."

Compared to that, loving a baby was a piece of cake. In a sudden rush of affection, Simon halted in his tracks, tugged the flour baby out of his bag, and sat down with her on his knee beside the creek.

"I'll tell you what I like about you," he said, staring into her big round eyes. "You're very easy to get along with. You're not like my mother, always telling me to put my plate in the sink, or shut doors more quietly, or pick my shoes up off the floor. You're not like Grandma, always telling me how much I've grown, and asking me what I'm going to do when I get out of school. You don't want me to be different, like all my teachers do. You don't tease me, like Sue. And you don't run off and leave, like my father."

Tucking her under his arm, he gazed out over the water.

"I wouldn't mind you being real," he said. "Even if it was more work. Even if you howled, and kept filling your diapers, and threw giant tantrums in stores. I wouldn't mind."

He peeped down at her, comfy and safe in his armpit, and pressed a finger where her nose would be, if she weren't just a bag of flour.

"I'll tell you what I don't understand," he confided. "I don't understand how people can treat babies badly."

Her huge eyes stared up at him. He tried to explain.

"Mom says she knows how it happens." Simon couldn't help scowling. "In fact, she says she wouldn't like to count the number of times I nearly got seriously rearranged by her, when I was teething."

He shook his head in amazement.

"And Grandma says her sister lost her temper once, and threw her baby in the crib so hard that one of its legs broke."

He bent his head closer.

"Not one of the baby's legs," he explained. "One of the crib's."

Glad to have made that clear, he pressed on.

"And Sue claims she gets so ratty if she doesn't get a full eight hours uninterrupted sleep every night that it's a good thing she never had a family because, if she did, she'd murder all of them within a week."

He pulled the flour baby onto his knee.

"And Mom went camping with Sue once, for only two nights, and came back saying she believed it."

He poked her gently where her tummy would be.

"And look at Robin," he said. "He's usually easy-going enough. He puts up with Mr. Cassidy picking on him about keeping his eraser dropping collection in his desk, and puts up with all Wayne's jokes about him having two left feet. It's not like Robin to go totally ape like that."

He stared over the flour baby's head, into the dark flowing water. It wasn't even, he thought, as if anything very special had happened to drive Robin wild. Certainly nothing to explain him seeing red like that, and getting in such a frenzy. All that had happened was that Warren had asked to borrow somebody's notebook.

"Why?"

"To copy yesterday's homework."

"You don't want mine, then," Wayne had said. "I got all of it wrong."

"You don't want mine either," George assured him. "Mr. Cassidy told me a brain-dead troll could have made a better stab at it."

To Warren, the actual quality of the work on offer was clearly a matter of total indifference.

"All Mr. Cassidy said was that I had to *do* it," he explained. "He didn't say anything about getting it *right*."

"You can borrow mine if you want," Robin offered. "He didn't say it was garbage, so I think he must have liked it."

"Fine," said Warren. "I'll take yours." And he

stood by while Robin dug in his bag, pushing aside his math textbook and the new French picture dictionary Mr. Dupasque had insisted on giving him only that morning. In search of the homework, he dug too deeply too fast, and his flour baby fell out on the muddy path.

"Oh, shoot!"

Picking it up, he brushed the worst of the mud and gravel off, and tossed it to Warren for safekeeping.

True to form, Warren dropped it.

It fell in the mud again. This time, Robin picked it up and stuck it firmly in a bush beside the path, before digging deeper in the bag. Above his own furious scrabblings, he didn't hear the soft ripping of the flour baby behind him. It was only when the little burlap bag had torn sufficiently to drop back in the mud with a soft floury splat that he even realized what was happening.

And that was the moment at which he lost his temper.

"Stupid!" he yelled. "Stupid! Stupid! Stupid!"

Warren stepped back nervously. Was he being blamed? But no. It was the flour baby that had put Robin in a rage. Picking it off the ground, he'd shaken it till flour spilled.

"Stupid! Stupid!" he yelled again, punching it hard.

Flour puffed out in clouds.

Robin went berserk.

"Take care of your flour baby!" he screamed, in

mimicry of all the adults who had been nagging him for days. "Don't forget! Take it here! Take it there! Make sure you strap it safely on your bike! Don't lose it! Keep it out of the mud!"

For every order he shouted, he gave the flour baby a hard punch.

"Don't let it get wet! Don't let it get dirty! Make sure it doesn't fall! Don't forget to pretend it's a real baby!"

Now he was shaking it so fiercely the rip widened, and flour spilled on the path.

"Pretend you're real! Fine! I'll pretend you're real! And if you were real, if you were mine, I'd kick you in the creek!"

And then, before their very eyes, he'd drawn back his foot, let go of the flour sack, and done it.

Thwack!

Simon sat quietly on the bank, remembering how, just as the damaged sack had sunk at once, the flour along the path had blown away in an instant. In less than a minute there was nothing to see except a few sad, rising bubbles.

He hugged his own flour baby tightly to his chest.

"I don't know much," he told her. "But I do know this. I'd never do that to you. Never, never, never."

And, at that moment, he believed himself.

CHAPTER 7

On Day 16, Mr. Cassidy couldn't do a thing with them. Philip Brewster fell off his chair arguing that the Chinese were the tallest people on earth. Luis Pereira kept pushing his desk out of line, over and over, till Mr. Cassidy realized Henry had convinced him that the spider on the ceiling just above his head was deadly poisonous, and also dribbling. Billy Simms wouldn't stop adding the most unpleasant flourishes to the huge bluebottle tattoo he'd inked on his forearm. And even Robin Delaney, who usually wasn't much trouble, kept flicking bits of his eraser dropping collection at the petunia on the windowsill.

"Right!" said Mr. Cassidy. "I know what we'll do. We'll have a few snippets from the diaries."

He waited for the groaning to peak.

"Or —" he threatened, "we could just have a second try at yesterday's disastrous test."

Everyone settled down hastily to listen to the diaries. Warren Meyer laid his head gently on his flour baby, as though it were a pillow on the desk. His eyes closed, and his thumb crept in his mouth. Nobody scoffed. It was as if they took it for a signal that today was time out. It was back to the nursery.

Within moments, everyone had spread themselves as comfortably as possible. Some of them even copied Simon by propping their flour babies on the desk tops, as if they were listening too.

Mr. Cassidy began.

"I'll start with Henry," he told them. "Henry on Day 9."

Henry's arm punched the air.

Mr. Cassidy began.

" 'I hate my flour baby. I hate it more than anything else on earth. It weighs about a ton. I asked my Dad how much I weighed when I was born, and he said he might have got me mixed up with Jim or Laura, but he thinks I weighed eight pounds. Eight pounds! That's another three on top of Fatso here! I asked Dad how much that was in kilos, and he went all snitty and said he cooked my supper and fixed my bike, I couldn't expect him to do my homework as well.' "

Mr. Cassidy broke off.

A faint roar of approval came from those members of the class who had both stayed awake and listened till the end.

"Now we'll have Tullis's," said Mr. Cassidy. "Since he's not here. This is Day 8. I should warn you, Days 2 to 7 and 9 to 13 are unaccountably missing."

He waited for the laughter to subside before reading out, with an expression of distaste:

> *" 'My flour baby has a booger down her front. I'm not flicking it off. It's not mine, so why should I?' "*

He stopped.
"That's it."

A cheer rose to greet this announcement. Encouraged, Mr. Cassidy picked up Rick Tullis's effort for Day 14.

> *" 'If I've been goofing off a lot, you can blame the flour baby. I'm not saying I would have bothered to come much anyway. But with that thing around, I'm definitely staying out again tomorrow.' "*

Mr. Cassidy lifted his head to gaze around the classroom.

"He's taken to numbering his sentences," he informed them. "In case he should make the terrible mistake of writing more than three."

He rooted through the pile of diary entries.

"Here's something interesting," he told them. "Two exactly the same."

He read the first aloud. It was by Wayne Driscoll.

" 'My mom says when I was born, we were so poor we practically lived in a bucket and ate rocks. This was because my grandpa said I looked like a goblin. Mom stopped speaking to him, so he wouldn't lend her any money. Mom thinks he was fed up because I'm black and he isn't. Not that he's my dad, just my grandad, so what's it to him? I bet my dad would have been a whole lot worse than fed up if I'd come out all white! Mom says she has no patience with either of them and wishes everyone in the world was green.' "

Picking up another, scruffier, piece of paper, Mr. Cassidy read the whole sorry tale out over again, word for word.

One by one, they all raised their heads to look at Warren Meyer.

"What's the matter?" Warren demanded. "Why are you all staring at me?"

"You can't just copy *anything*," Robin Delaney explained kindly. "It has to make sense for *you*. And you're not *black*."

Warren took to muttering. Very little was audible, except to his nearest neighbors. But some approximation to the phrase 'racial discrimination' could be heard coming up now and then in the course of his grumbling.

Mr. Cassidy ignored him.

"Shall we move on?" he asked pleasantly. "Let's have Tyrone Schumaker on Day 14."

Tyrone stared around the room proudly, inviting admiration. A few of them took the trouble to scowl, but most pretended that they hadn't noticed him.

> " 'By today, I should have made well over
> a hundred dollars, but what with six people
> not putting their flour babies in my day
> care, and Tullis forever goofing off, and
> me not thinking to start until Day 4, and
> some people not coughing up what they
> owe me in spite of having Henry and Billy
> set on them, I only have half of that so far.
> Still —' "

Mr. Cassidy stopped on the upbeat, and waited for everyone to guess the end.

"*That's business!*" roared everyone, in unison.

Mr. Cassidy took time out to run his eyes over Tyrone's work a second time.

"There's only two sentences here," he warned.

Over and above Tyrone's prolonged and furious disputation with Mr. Cassidy about the exact nature and role of the comma, some serious accusations could be heard from the others.

". . . robbing us *blind!*"

". . . chiseled me out of four weeks' allowance already!"

". . . *never* get around to paying him back at this rate . . ."

"Good as stealing, frankly . . ."

Mr. Cassidy shifted uncomfortably on the desk. Waving Tyrone into silence, he reminded the others:

"Nobody forced you to put your flour babies into his day care."

Then, hastily, he picked up another sheet of paper. "Here's Simon," he told them. "Simon on Day 12.

> *'I was really upset by Delaney booting his flour baby in the creek like that. I never thought of Delaney as a hard nugget before. In fact, he's a really good friend of mine. I expect that his problem is what Miss Arnott's always saying. He's rather immature.' "*

Mr. Cassidy raised his head from the paper in order to interrupt himself and say to Simon:

"I hope you realize that reading all this out so smoothly and evenly is a real triumph of the decipherer's art."

Not really grasping the full force of Mr. Cassidy's insult, Simon contented himself with a sour grunt, which Mr. Cassidy chose to take as permission to carry on reading.

> *" 'My mom kept sticking up for Robin too. She said you can't go around giving people The Black Spot just because they do*

something stupid, or I'd still be marked
down for a sinner for throwing that cactus at
Hyacinth Spicer, or giving Tullis's German
shepherd my grandma's wig to chew, and
one or two other things I don't really want to
write about in this diary.' "

Unfortunately for Simon, George O'Rourke did
not seem to share his very acute sense of privacy.

"I think he means the time he flushed his geography project away, and flooded all the johns," he confided to everyone.

"No," said Tariq. "He means the time he fed Miss Arnott's aspirin to the gerbil, and the poor thing ended up in a coma."

He looked around, to check that no one had misunderstood.

"Not Miss Arnott," he said, just in case doubt was lingering in anyone's mind. "The gerbil."

"No, no, no." Impatiently, Wayne brushed Tariq's theory aside. "He means the time he used that big red DANGER sign as a leg-up to get over the wire fence, and got caught leaning against that huge gas cylinder, having a quiet cigarette."

By now, Mr. Cassidy was eyeing Simon with a new respect. A huge hunk of a lad, yes. And strong. But what he'd never realized before was what a swathe of mayhem the boy left behind as he shambled through life.

Then, suddenly noticing everyone looking at him

expectantly, Mr. Cassidy felt obliged to come up with some suitably pedagogic response.

"You shouldn't smoke," he scolded Simon. "You might stunt your growth."

And he went on to Philip Brewster, Day 10.

" 'Bad times! I thought my flour baby was the pits, but the people next door have a real one and it's a yowler. On and on and on. I hear it through the wall. As I told Trish, my goldfish, if it were mine, I'd tie its neck in a reef knot.' "

Fascinated, Mr. Cassidy shuffled through the pages till he found Philip Brewster, Day 11.

" 'What gets me is that I get a serious roasting for playing my radio so soft I can't even hear it. This baby is switched up to Volume 10 all night, and when I come down in the morning firing on only one cylinder because I've had no sleep, everyone tells me we're lucky it isn't our baby. I wish it were. I'd soon put an end to its bleating.' "

Everyone turned to look at Philip, who blushed.

"Go on," Tariq begged Mr. Cassidy. "Go on with the story, sir. Find his Day 12."

Mr. Cassidy found Philip's Day 12.

" 'I went around and told that woman next door I wasn't getting much sleep, and she went totally unravelled. I only just managed

*to get off the doorstep ahead of the lava. I
don't understand people with babies, I
really don't.' "*

A warm, full-throated cheer of agreement greeted
this last announcement.

"Yeah! People with babies have to be totally unhinged."

"Crazy as coots."

It was Tyrone, as usual, who put the point over
most coherently.

"I mean, they stroll around all day with these real
ones tucked under their arms that keep bawling and
messing and having to have their butts wiped —"

"Not just their butts!" interrupted Henry. "My
mom says you have to keep wiping their noses."

"Grotesque!"

"Disgusting!"

"Just the thought of it makes you feel *sick*."

"And then they yowl all night!"

A fresh onset of grumbling from the back row
proved to be Philip Brewster's personal corrobora-
tion of this last complaint.

"That's all I said to her, that it had been yowling
all night. And she went *berserk*."

Tyrone went on with his allegations.

"And some of them are even heavier than ours. My
aunt brings hers around and it weighs twenty-four
pounds. Twenty-four pounds! And my aunt still has
to carry it. It still can't walk!"

Wayne Driscoll broke in at this point.

"That's definitely the thing that gets me about them. They can't walk. They can't talk. They can't kick a ball, or even get the spoon anywhere near their own faces."

"They're just a total nuisance."

"You can't blame Robin for booting his in the creek."

"His flour baby was *lucky*," Tariq told them darkly. "In the good old days, people used to dump babies out on the mountainside."

"Or cook and eat them."

Mr. Cassidy felt obliged to step in at this point to pull the lively class discussion back on the rails.

"No, I don't think so, George. Not cook and eat them."

"Oh yes, sir." George was adamant. "They taste exactly like pork. I read it in a book."

The general clamor for more information was almost drowned out by potential individual researchers.

"What book?"

"Do you still have it?"

"Can I borrow it?"

"*Pork?*"

"What about ribs? Do babies make good ribs?"

Hastily, Mr. Cassidy spoke up again.

"People with babies aren't all totally insane," he told them. "In fact, any one of you might choose to have one some day. Not to mention the fact that many people end up with babies by accident."

The rush of feeling engendered by this observation astonished even Mr. Cassidy.

"That's *terrible!*"

"Having a baby by accident!"

"Seriously stricken!"

"I'd *never* have one by accident. Never!"

Billy Simms seemed almost in tears at the idea.

"It's horrible even to think about. One careless moment and then — hell on wheels!"

Warren clearly agreed with him.

"Your whole life ruined by *one slip*."

"Shocking!"

Luis Pereira took full advantage of his reputation for knowing more girls than anyone else in the class.

"And it might not even be your fault," he warned them all conspiratorially.

There was sheer consternation at the thought that anyone present might end up with a baby through no real fault of his own. For the second time in under three weeks, Room 8 fell absolutely silent.

Spike Moranis rose to his feet.

"Suppose —"

Words failed him.

Mr. Cassidy looked at him encouragingly.

"Yes, son?"

"Suppose —"

Once again, Spike couldn't carry on.

Mr. Cassidy looked blank. But all the others were clearly finding it easier to interpret the look of baffled horror on Spike's face.

"Yes! Yes! Spike is right! Suppose you get stuck —"

"*With* someone —"

"And you're not absolutely sure —"

"Might not be safe."

"You can always say no," Wayne Driscoll responded virtuously.

The others seemed satisfied with this.

"That's right."

"Just say no."

"Not worth taking any risks," Phil Brewster told them all sagely.

"Better be safe than sorry."

"One sloppy moment, and your life's not your own."

Mr. Cassidy gazed out at the worried faces, all struggling with the idea of having to defend themselves against the terrible dangers on the horizon. Only one member of the class didn't seem swept up in the general anxiety, and that was Simon Martin. Simon was sitting chewing his pen, and staring thoughtfully out of the window. He'd been quiet throughout the whole hubbub. Mr. Cassidy was pretty sure he understood why Simon hadn't joined in the general pillorying of the flour babies. After all, he'd taken such a strong shine to his own that his psychology had been a matter of heated discussion for over two weeks now during the lunch hour, with half of the teachers insisting the poor boy was in dire need of professional counseling, and the rest lining up behind Mr. Dupasque and Miss Arnott to claim his response was "rather sweet," and more to be applauded than pitied.

But what was he thinking now? What was on his mind?

Deliberately, Mr. Cassidy picked out the semiliterate Spike Moranis to read the names on top of the diary entries and distribute them back to their owners. Then, under the cover of the spreading riot, he slid off his desk and made his way around the class until he was beside Simon and could ask him privately:

"A penny for your thoughts?"

Simon glanced up.

"I was just thinking about my father," he said.

Mr. Cassidy gave this response a moment's consideration. You had to be careful. These days, some parents swapped spouses around like new computer games, or football cards. Only the week before, he'd strolled behind a couple of pupils working side by side, and heard one saying to the other, amiably enough: "You've got my old dad now, haven't you?" No, you had to be very much on your guard.

"Do you have a new one I don't yet know about?" he asked Simon politely.

"No," Simon said. "I was thinking about my real one. I can't help wondering about him. He's on my mind."

Mr. Cassidy trod as carefully as he could.

"Is there anything in particular bothering you?"

"Yes. Yes, there is," said Simon. "There's something I really want to know."

Mr. Cassidy pitched his voice over the growing tumult behind them.

"What?"

"What he was whistling."

Mr. Cassidy was mystified.

"What he was whistling?"

"When he left," Simon explained. "I want to know what he was whistling the day he walked out."

Mr. Cassidy was floored. After a moment, he patted Simon affectionately on the shoulder.

"Sorry, son," he said gently. "Not on the syllabus."

He was on the verge of adding, under his breath: "Nothing of much use is," when suddenly it struck him he didn't mean it and it wasn't true. They'd learned a lot from this science fair project, for example. Dr. Devoy was right. They'd learned about the tedium of responsibility, its endless grind, and how they felt about it. Mild little Robin Delaney had even learned he had a serious temper. Tyrone had learned (if he didn't know already) he had a healthy entrepreneurial streak. And every single one of them now knew that, old enough to father a baby as he might be, he was not yet old enough to be a father.

Every single one of them?

Maybe not. Mr. Cassidy still had his doubts about Simon. There the lad sat, his huge limbs folded uncomfortably under his desk, fingering the gray lace on his flour baby's bonnet and sunk morosely in thought.

Was he still wondering about his father? Or was he, as half the teachers insisted, going broody with longing for a real baby of his own?

Either way, it was time to put a stop to it. Mr. Cassidy had never claimed to be a patient man. And it was at this moment that he decided he'd had enough. There was, after all, almost a whole year of teaching the boy still ahead. He couldn't stand this woebegone face, these glum looks. Up until now, Mr. Cassidy had not really noticed that many compensations came his way for having to teach in Room 8. But now he saw that most of them, even if they weren't all that bright, did at least make the effort to stay chirpy. Wasn't there some old sea song about being of good cheer?

Kill two birds with one stone, thought Mr. Cassidy.

Reaching down, he snatched Simon's flour baby off the desk, and put it behind his back, where Simon couldn't see it. Only when he was sure he had the boy's full attention did he say:

"I'll tell you what your dad was whistling."

The tone of utter confidence with which Mr. Cassidy made this pronouncement caused Simon's eyes to widen.

"When he walked out, your dad was whistling 'Sail Away,'" Mr. Cassidy told the boy with utter finality. "That's what he was whistling: 'Sail Away.'"

He didn't hang around for Simon to start asking how he knew, or ask him to hum the melody or remember the words. He simply dropped Simon's flour baby back on the desk, and took off as fast as a man of his bulk could go, across the room, not even slowing up to pull the occasional pair of pugilists in the aisle apart, or tell Luis to stop chipping at his desktop.

He didn't stop until he reached his desk.

"Right!" he bellowed. "That's it. I've had enough. It's nearly time, so clear out, the whole pack of you. Go home."

This precipitated the usual tiresome performance, but in reverse this time.

"But, sir! Sir! The bell hasn't rung yet!"

"Just go, Tariq. Go home, all of you, before I change my mind."

He sat watching the usual riot and confusion that took place as they poured out. Simon wasn't the first to reach the door, he noticed; but neither was he by any means the last. And the troubled look on his face had vanished. The power was back in his stride.

Content, Mr. Cassidy started to pack his own briefcase, ready to take off for home. Not a bad lesson for Room 8, he thought. Not bad. Not bad.

Contrary to expectation — against all odds — he'd managed to do something with them.

CHAPTER

"**Go on,**" said Simon. "Sing it."

"I can't." Simon's mother turned to catch Ruggles creeping up on the flour baby, and swatted him with the dish towel. "You know I can't sing."

"I'm not planning to give you a grade," Simon assured her. "I just want to hear the words and learn the tune."

"I don't know all the words. I'm not even sure I'd get the tune right."

"Go on," Simon insisted. "Have a try."

So Mrs. Martin had a try. Wiping her hands dry, she leaned back against the sink, and, while Simon rocked the flour baby in his arms, deliberately provoking Ruggles into yelping spasms of jealousy, she sang out as bravely as she could.

"Unfurl the sail, lads, and let the winds find me
Breasting the soft, sunny, blue rising main —"

She broke off.
Simon looked up.

"Well?" he demanded. "What's the problem?"

"I've forgotten the next part."

Simon sighed with exasperation.

"But that was only *two lines*. You only sang *two lines*."

Mrs. Martin threw the dish towel at Ruggles, who was surreptitiously taking advantage of the lull in the rocking to chew a bit more off one of the flour baby's corners.

"Two lines is all I can remember."

"Pathetic," said Simon.

He looked so morose, Mrs. Martin felt sorry for him.

"Maybe the rest will come back to me," she tried to console him.

But Simon wasn't in the mood for waiting.

"I know," he said. "We'll call Sue."

Dumping the flour baby on the seat of the chair, he made for the telephone.

Shaking her head, Mrs. Martin asked her son:

"And why should Sue know the words?"

He didn't dare suggest that if it was the song his father had been whistling the very last time Sue ever saw him, then she might very well have tucked little snatches of it away in her brain.

He thrust the phone at his mother.

"Just call and ask."

"Don't be silly, Simon," said Mrs. Martin.

She reached down to pry the flour baby out from between Ruggles's teeth as, seizing his chance, he tried to slink past her to the door. "I can't just call Sue and ask her to sing over the phone."

"Why not?"

Put to the test, Mrs. Martin couldn't think of any reason. So while Simon used a clean pair of underpants from the laundry pile to try to wipe the worst of Ruggles's slobber off the flour baby, she made the call.

And Sue, when she answered, didn't seem to find the request at all strange. Even before Simon could snatch the phone from his mother's ear, and put it to his own, he could hear her chirruping away down the line.

"Toss all my burdens and woes clear behind me,
Vow I'll not carry those cargoes again."

Then, just like his mother, Sue broke off.

"I've forgotten the chorus," she told him. "Something about sunrise, and being of good cheer."

It was only the warning look on his mother's face that turned Simon's howl of frustration into a meager grunt of thanks. Handing the phone back, he banged his fist against the kitchen door in sheer irritation, and then, when it flew open, felt obliged to walk through, because his mother was still watching him.

In the shared yard, Hyacinth Spicer was sitting daintily on an upturned bucket, dyeing her sandals green. Hyacinth probably knew the whole song, Simon thought moodily. Learned it at Brownies, brushed it up at Little Woodland Folk, and sang the descant in the Baptist church choir. But he'd be happily boiled in oil before he'd ask Hyacinth Spicer any favors. He already suspected her of being one of Mr. Cassidy's spies: a good amateur turned professional. He was on the verge of turning back into the house when Hyacinth herself raised the topic spontaneously.

"Was that your mom singing?" she asked. Then, dabbing dye carefully on her sandal strap, "Not very good, is she?"

An idea struck Simon. It was worth a try, anyway.

"It's a very hard song to sing," he said.

Hyacinth looked up in surprise.

"No, it isn't."

"Of course it is," Simon insisted. "The chorus is particularly tricky."

"No, it isn't."

And, her capacity for showing off undimmed since the day Miss Ness first pinned the huge tinfoil star of Bethlehem to her sweater in nursery school, Hyacinth threw back her head and sang:

> "*Sail for a sunrise that burns with new maybes,*
> *Farewell, my loved ones, and be of good cheer.*
> *Others may settle to dandle their babies —*"

Just at that moment, she glanced down and noticed the dye dripping into her sandal.

"Oh, sh — ugar!"

Simon tried tempting her into singing what he could tell, from the sheer swell of the melody, must be the one, last, elusive line.

"You probably dripped that deliberately," he said. "Since it's the end of the song that's the hardest to sing well."

But Hyacinth Spicer had completely lost interest. She was intent on mopping up her shoe.

"Take a hike, Simon," she told him, just softly enough for both of them to be able to pretend he hadn't heard.

Simon went back inside. Shutting the door carefully, so Hyacinth Spicer couldn't hear, he sang what he'd learned of the chorus to his mother. But though she claimed then, and several times later that evening, that the last line was on the tip of her tongue, she never managed to come out with it.

By morning, Simon was in the sort of mental state he associated with victims of the water-drip torture.

"I'm going crazy," he told his mother over breakfast. "It's driving me insane."

"You could go and be nice to Hyacinth. She'd sing you the last line."

The scowl Simon turned on her was prodigious.

Mrs. Martin shrugged.

"Then you'll just have to ask Mr. Cassidy."

Ask Mr. Cassidy! Simon shoveled more cereal in his mouth, and used the freshly licked spoon to poke the flour baby.

"This is your fault," he told her. And it was. If it

weren't for her, he realized, he would never have started to take an interest in his father, and what happened years ago. Without this stupid, useless, floppy bag of flour, he'd never have ended up in the awful, shaming position he was in today — eager to get off to school to learn something, like a real earhole!

He prodded the flour baby again. This time, a few drops of muddy brown milk from his bran cereal slid off his spoon and slithered down her front.

"You'll catch it," his mother warned him cheerily. "Look at the poor little soul. Slobber, toothmarks, bran smears. And that's just the last five minutes."

"She's all right," Simon said shortly. He poked her again. "Aren't you?"

The flour baby didn't demur. But peering more closely as he shoved her away in his bag, Simon could see that she was hardly in a state to pass muster at the twice-weekly weigh-in. Not only had she become grimy beyond belief over the last few days, but her corners were frayed and her bottom was leaking.

Simon gave her the look that never failed to send Miss Arnott scurrying for her aspirin. How could something that couldn't even walk get into such a mess? What a major pain!

And now his mother was handing him a plastic bag.

"You'd better take this for her," she warned. "The forecast is rain."

He could have pointed out that any rainwater that fell on the flour baby might clean her up a bit, or make up some weight from the leakage. But, frankly, he couldn't be bothered. He was sick of the whole business.

Forcing the last spoonfuls of bran into his already bulging cheeks, he made a noise he hoped his mother would be charitable enough to take for a good-bye, and scooped up his school things and his flour baby.

Mrs. Martin stood firmly between him and the door.

"Good-bye, Simon," she said pointedly.

His mouth still stuffed to bursting, he grunted again.

She stood her ground.

"Good-bye, Simon," she repeated patiently.

He recognized it for the yellow card.

He stood there, like a huge dummy, making the effort to chew and swallow his huge mouthful of bran.

Then:

"Bye, Mom."

She smiled at last, letting him off the hook. He took off down the walk, leaving the door swinging on its hinges. Strange, he was thinking, how parents, like teachers, could keep up the nagging for years and years about stupid little things like saying thank you and good-bye. He didn't know how they did it. He'd go crazy within a week. Every single morning he went through this performance with his mother about emptying his mouth and saying good-bye properly. Every single school morning! That was five times a week, four weeks a month, several months a year. Every year. How many times was that? Millions, at least. So how did she manage to stand there each day and go through the whole thing without flying off the handle and going at him with a meat-axe? He certainly wouldn't manage it, that was for sure. He thought of himself as patient as the next man. But if he had to remind the flour baby more than a dozen times in a row about not leaving the back door wide open, or turning off the hot water faucet, or talking with her mouth full, he'd do a Delaney and boot her straight in the creek. Maybe the reason why his father left was that, like Simon, he realized almost right away he wasn't up to the job.

Reaching the end of Washington Street, Simon unaccountably burst into song.

"*Others may settle to dandle their babies —*" he warbled lustily, as, rounding the corner, he tripped over Wayne Driscoll, who was messing around in the gutter.

"What are you doing in there?" Simon asked, picking himself up, and loath to believe the evidence of his own eyes, since Wayne appeared to be stooped over a grating, scooping up dirt and trickling it between his fingers into his flour baby through a small tear in the fabric.

Wayne's brows were knitted in the fiercest concentration.

"Hold it steady for me, Sime. I can't get this dirt down the little hole."

127 •

Simon squatted in the gutter and took Wayne's bag of flour from him.

"You could make the hole bigger," he suggested.

Wayne snorted.

"Oh, ace idea, Sime! Give Old Hopalong *two* reasons to maul me!"

With his free hand, Simon tipped his own flour baby out of his bag.

"If you're in trouble, so am I," he said. "Mine looks a lot worse than yours."

Wayne took a break from trickling dirt to glance at Simon's flour baby.

"Jeez, Sime! What a grime-bag! You'll catch it this morning."

"No, I won't," Simon said confidently. Then, slightly less sure, he took another look. Maybe he would. No doubt about it, his flour baby was a mess. How had it happened? How did she get so mucky so quickly? One moment Simon was Star of the Project, with teachers he barely knew nodding affectionately at him in the corridors. The next, he was carrying around a grungy, leaking sack of flour with two smudged eyes and chewed corners. What went wrong?

"You should never have let Hooper and Meyer use her as a goal marker," Wayne was telling him.

Simon defended himself as best he could.

"That didn't make much difference. What got her so torn was using her to tease Hyacinth Spicer's cat."

"I don't think the rips look nearly as bad as the chewed parts," Wayne observed dispassionately.

"I blame Ruggles," Simon said gloomily. "He's had it in for my flour baby since the very first day."

"What about those black smudges?"

"Fell in the fireplace."

"And the scurfy black charred parts?"

"Oh, those are my fault," Simon admitted. "I left her too near the stove burner while I fried hamburger."

"What about all this stuff stuck to her butt?"

Simon upturned her, and inspected her.

"Glue," he said. "Lump of bubble gum. Mud. Ruggles's dried slobber. Chicken noodle soup —"

There was enough to keep the litany up for quite a while. But, hastily, Wayne interrupted him.

"Come on, Sime. Time to go."

And confident that, at the very least, he wouldn't come off worst at the morning inspection, Wayne pulled Simon with him along the street. As they reached the rotary, Simon took to explaining the problem he had with the flour baby.

"I'm not the type, you see. I thought I was, at first. But it turned out I was wrong. Some people are good at looking after things. Some people aren't. I guess I'm out of the second box. More like my dad."

Wayne shot him a curious look, making Simon realize it must be the very first time his friend had ever heard him bring up the subject of his father. But he pressed on anyway.

"He couldn't handle it either, that's obvious. Maybe some people can't. Maybe they're just like that, and you can't blame them."

As usual, he stepped out fearlessly into the stream of cars slowing unwillingly for the rotary.

"He just wasn't the sort to settle and dandle his babies," he yelled, over the roar of the traffic.

As usual, Wayne scurried in his wake, nodding apologetically to all the drivers Simon had just brought screeching to a halt.

"Wasn't the sort to *what?*"

But Simon was over the road now, and striding purposefully across the grass toward the school building. There was one last thing he wanted to find out, one last clue to the mystery of his father's disappearance. One thing he still needed to know.

"Miss Arnott! Miss Arnott!"

She turned as soon as she heard him.

"What is it, Simon?"

To her astonishment, he started to sing at her in the rich, robust, unembarrassed tenor voice she'd heard often enough in Assembly, and never realized belonged to him.

"*Unfurl the sail, lads, and let the winds find me —*"

"Simon?"

"*Breasting the soft, sunny, blue rising main —*"

Was he trying to get a rise out of her?

"I'm in a hurry, Simon," she told him, as a warning. But he kept pace with her along the path, still singing heartily.

"*Toss all my burdens and woes clear behind me —*"

"Is this a joke, Simon? A bet? A sponsored sing?"

"*Vow I'll not carry those cargoes again.*"

• 130

Impatient, she turned away, along the narrower path that led to the teachers' door. Totally ignoring the strict school rule, and the sign on the little wooden post: *Teachers Only Beyond This Point*, Simon charged along beside her, still singing his powerful heart out.

> *"Sail for a sunrise that burns with new maybes,*
> *Farewell, my loved ones —"*

Miss Arnott stopped in her tracks. She'd never faced this problem with Simon before. Moody and awkward he could be. And downright troublesome on some occasions. But she had to admit that, in all her experience of the boy, she'd never known him to be truly disobedient. What should she do? Tackle him? Or ignore it? First things first, thought Miss Arnott. Who was watching?

She glanced up to where, framed in the teachers' room window, Mr. Cassidy was blowing the smoke of his last surreptitious cigarette before class out from between the blinds.

He gave a little wave, then, taking her look of temporary indecision for one of pitiful entreaty, he threw up the sash window, all set to bellow at Simon for daring to set foot on hallowed turf.

"— *and be of good cheer*," he heard Simon singing at the top of his voice.

Be of good cheer? The snatch of song rang a bell instantly in Mr. Cassidy's brain. He couldn't help staring down at Simon with a teacherly blend of pleasure and pride. What price psychology now? Why, the lad was a walking tribute to good old-fashioned horse sense. Look at the change in him, for heaven's sake. One morning he was moping around like a fool, in love with his revolting little sack of flour. A word in his ear from his wise old class teacher, and look at him. Right back to normal (well, normal for *him,* of course), and courting the only real love of his life, the heavenly Miss Arnott, in fine voice, and full throttle.

"*Others may settle to dandle their babies —*" Simon's glorious warm tenor rang out, over the grounds.

The pause that followed lasted a beat too long. It was, Mr. Cassidy thought, a bit like that old oriental torture of waiting for the water drip.

When he could stand it no longer, he threw the window up higher, leaned out and roared in the great, tuneful baritone he used to haul them back to time in hymns:

"*My heart's a tall ship, and high winds are near.*"

Simon dropped to his knees, exhausted. Miss Arnott fled. And Wayne came thumping up behind.

"What was Old Hopalong bellowing about?"

"*My heart's a tall ship,*" panted Simon. "*And high winds are near.*"

Wayne made a face.

"What's that supposed to mean?"

Simon looked up to ask Mr. Cassidy. But it was

too late. Perfectly content with the satisfactory rounding off of a lovely old sea song, Mr. Cassidy had stubbed out his cigarette, pulled down the window, and vanished.

As had been proved more than once on the soccer field, dogged determination was one of Wayne's most salient characteristics.

"How can a heart be a tall ship?" he persisted.

"I don't know, do I?" snapped Simon. "We'll have to ask someone."

"Who?"

Wayne looked around. The only person in sight was Martin Simon, who was strolling along the path reading *The Quest for the Holy Grail*.

"Ask him. He's an earhole. He might know."

Simon's face brightened. Yes, Martin Simon might know. Anyone who puffed around all day reading poetry — often in French — was bound to have no trouble putting a fancy line of a song into plain English. No trouble at all.

Simon picked himself off his knees, and walked over the grass, till he was almost directly in front of Martin. Sticking out his foot, he waited calmly and deliberately until Martin tripped over it, and *The Quest for the Holy Grail* fell out of his hand onto the grass.

"Sorry," said Simon, stooping to pick it up and hand it back.

"Thanks," Martin said, somewhat warily.

But Simon felt that, by reaching down to pick up

the book, he had already established his good faith. There was no need for any further tact.

"Look," he said. "You're an earhole. You read poetry. What does it mean if someone says they're a tall ship?"

Martin hesitated. It could be the start of a tease. But, on the other hand, there was a serious and determined look about Simon, as if, like Sir Galahad in the book that he'd just handed back, he was on some sort of quest.

"A tall ship?"

"Yes, a tall ship."

You had to hand it to these brain boxes, Simon reflected as he stood waiting for the answer. If anyone strolled up to him and asked him a question like that, he'd push them in the face and stride off. But Martin didn't seem to find it either odd or insulting to be asked a question about what might even be a poem. He simply took off his glasses and wiped them while he had a little think, then asked:

"What did this person say *exactly?*"

No point in beating around the bush, thought Simon. So, throwing back his head, he sang out full-throatedly:

"*Others may settle to dandle their babies,*
My heart's a tall ship, and high winds are near."

Martin's look of confusion cleared instantly.

"Well, obviously it's a metaphor," he began. "The protagonist has chosen to use the analogy of —"

He stopped, partly from terror, and partly because Simon's sudden grip on his throat had cut off the air in his windpipe.

"I wasn't asking for a *lecture*," Simon informed him sternly. "I just want to know what it *means*."

He took his hand away, and stood waiting.

Martin Simon tried again.

"What it *means*," he said, "is that the fellow has to go. Just as a ship with its sails spread has to move with the winds, so this man knows the moment is coming when, however much he may *want* to stay, the sort of person he is — the sort of character and temperament he has — is going to force him to leave. He has no choice."

Simon stared up at the sky. His eyes were prickling, and he swallowed hard.

"No choice?"

Martin said firmly:

"None at all. That's just the way it is with someone like him."

At this point, Wayne broke in, asking Martin suspiciously:

"How can you be so sure?"

"It's in the *words*," Martin explained patiently. "That's what they *mean*."

"But how do you *know*?"

It was Simon who came to Martin's rescue, putting Wayne firmly in his place.

"Listen," he said. "You and me, we know how to play soccer and have a good laugh, right? Now Martin here, he's an earhole. He's useless at soccer. He couldn't kick Jell-O in a drain. But he knows about things like songs and poetry."

He turned to Martin.

"Isn't that right?"

Martin nodded.

"Right," Simon said. And then, since the discussion of cultural strengths and weaknesses seemed to have petered to a halt:

"Well, thanks a lot."

On an impulse, he stuck out his right arm. For just a moment Martin couldn't fathom why, and then he realized Simon wanted to shake hands with him.

"That's all right," he said, responding as promptly as he could. "Any time."

"No," Simon assured him. "That's it, I guess. I'm pretty sure I'll be all right now."

And indeed, Martin couldn't help thinking, there was a strange, unearthly look about him once again, almost an aura, as if, like Sir Galahad, he'd seen his vision of the Holy Grail, and knew he'd come across his heart's desire.

CHAPTER 9

Miss Arnott rummaged in her bag for aspirin.

"That's the third time he's tramped past this door, singing at the top of his voice." She turned to Father Maguire, who was hunched over the teachers' room work table, erasing the penciled black centers out of most of the quarter notes in the song books to try and turn them back into half notes. "Why can't you teach them quieter songs?"

Without raising his eyes from his salvage work, Father Maguire defended himself calmly.

"I never taught him that one. And what you teach them makes no difference. Those lads in Room 8 would belt out a lullaby as if it were a battle hymn. There's nothing I can do about it. Just thank your lucky stars the boy has a fine voice."

Miss Arnott dropped a second aspirin in her water glass.

"Call it a teacher's rest period," she muttered bitterly. "It's just a different way of suffering."

She lifted her head.

"Is that him coming back again? I can't *bear* it. What is the boy doing, traipsing up and down this hallway, time and again?"

Mr. Stoutamire broke off sipping coffee to tell her.

"If it's Simon Martin you're complaining about," he said, "Dr. Devoy roped him in to carry Ralph Fishbein's Microprocessor Controlled Pedestrian Crossing down to its stand for the Science Fair. For once, the boy's only doing what he's told."

"Was he told to sing sea shanties at full tilt while he did it?"

"Shall I tell him to turn down the volume?" Mr. Stoutamire stuck his head around the door, but he was a moment too late. Mr. Cassidy had already appeared at the other end of the corridor.

"Simon Martin!" he bellowed, cutting the enthusiastic tenor off at source. "Why aren't you down here at our weigh-in?"

Simon stopped short with his arms full of oscilloscope.

"I'm carrying stuff for Dr. Devoy, sir," he answered in the virtuous tones of one who knows himself to be girded with the strength of a more powerful teacher. "It's for the Science Fair."

Mr. Cassidy's face darkened. Science Fair! Science Fair! There was still half a week before it even started, and already he was heartily sick of it. Why, the business disrupted the whole semester. If every other school in creation could tack this sort of licensed chaos onto the very last week, why on earth couldn't

Dr. Devoy? Really, the man was getting too big for his boots.

Mutiny rose in Mr. Cassidy. Before he could stop himself, a string of unteacherly words sprang from his lips and rang down the corridor with such force that Simon was shocked. Not that he hadn't used language as bad as that himself. Worse, in fact. And quite often. But for Old Hopalong to start frothing at the mouth, and let fly with such a blue flood — well!

Simon gazed at his teacher with a new respect.

"And as for you!" Mr. Cassidy finished up, glowering horribly at Simon. "You can just put down that pile of junk, and come back to the classroom for the weigh-in."

"Yes, sir."

Simon laid the oscilloscope and Wishart's Digital Sine Wave Generator down on the floor, and submissively fell in behind as his teacher strode off down the corridor.

"That's better," muttered Mr. Cassidy. All very well, he was thinking, this business of Simon being in good cheer. But unfortunately, just like anything else in a school, it could be taken just that bit too far.

His bad mood lasted as far as the classroom.

"That's it!" he bellowed, as he came through the door in time to catch Philip Brewster practicing scissor jumps over Tyrone's baby carriages. "I've had enough! You can just push that tin juggernaut in the corner and line up with your little sacks of flour. I'm taking them in, and giving them back to Dr. Devoy."

"Giving them *back?*"

Mr. Cassidy totally misunderstood the nature of their astonishment and concern.

"Yes. Giving them back. I know it's four days too early, but you can just spend the time getting your diaries up to date."

"But —"

"No buts!" roared Mr. Cassidy. "Just get your flour babies, please, everyone."

He stood beside the scales.

"Who wants to be first?"

From the thunderstruck silence that followed, he took it that no one wanted to be first.

"How about you, George?"

George was too baffled even to shake his head.

"Henry?"

Henry looked to the others to sort out this obvious oversight. But, seeing him turn away, Mr. Cassidy moved on impatiently.

"What about Rick. Not here? No, of course not. What about you, then, Spike? Are you ready to hand over your flour sack? One last weighing, and the thing will be off your hands forever. How does that sound?"

Spike glanced up from picking cat hairs off his flour baby. He didn't realize that, by now, everyone else in the class was staring at Simon Martin expectantly, waiting for the one amongst them who had first burst in extolling the virtues of this particular experiment to break out of his ashen-faced paralysis and clear up this obvious confusion about the way it should end. Returning his attention to picking off the cat hairs, Spike simply asked:

"But what about the Glorious Explosion?"

Mr. Cassidy stared.

"The Glorious *What?*"

"The Glorious Explosion." Spike looked up again. "Simon told us that, on the last day, there'd be a glorious explosion. We'd all get to kick our flour babies to pieces."

"Kick them to pieces?"

Mr. Cassidy could scarcely hide his amusement. "Kick the flour babies to pieces? And you believed him?"

He looked around and saw all their crestfallen expressions.

"You did!" he declared. "You all believed him!"

He turned to Simon, whose stupefaction was giving way to deep embarrassment.

"You managed to convince them that, on the last day, they'd get to kick over a hundred pounds of sifted white flour around?"

Simon nodded.

Mr. Cassidy spread his arms wide.

"Here? In my classroom?"

Simon nodded again.

And then, slowly, seismically, Mr. Cassidy began chuckling. As he gripped the sides of his desk to steady himself, the chuckling grew. It grew from chuckles into loud guffaws, and from guffaws into huge rocking laughter. From huge rocking laughter it became an earthquake of merriment. Tears of amusement flooded from his eyes. The desk beneath him pitched and rolled. The windows rattled in their frames, and, next door, Miss Arnott feared for her wall display.

Mr. Cassidy pointed at Simon.

"You — You —"

For quite a while, he couldn't get it out.

"You told them they would be allowed to kick one hundred pounds of sifted white flour around in my classroom!"

He fished in his jacket pocket and drew out his huge spotted handkerchief. He wiped his streaming eyes.

"And they believed you!"

Still laughing fit to burst, he fell off his desk and landed on the floor. The boards shook. The desk careered over backwards, snapping the steel-tipped wooden blackboard rule in two, trapping one half beneath, and sending the other flying up at the ceiling, where it hit the central light fixture.

BANG!!!!!!

There was a glorious explosion. Showers of sparks and splintered glass rained down on them, and their gasps of astonishment and delight were drowned by the hissing and spitting of ancient and overstressed electrical wiring.

The silence that followed was palpable. Then,

"See?" Robin said loyally. "Simon was right."

Loyally, too, he went off with his friend, to fetch the broom and the dustpan. Together they swept the shards of glass into a neat pile behind the door, and set Mr. Cassidy's desk back on its legs.

Mr. Cassidy set the scales down.

"Fine," he said. "Joke's over."

He pointed at Spike, as the nearest.

"Hand over your flour baby."

Not knowing what else to do, Spike passed his flour baby to Mr. Cassidy, who dumped it on the scale.

"Not bad, Spike. It's only lost a tiny bit of weight, and, apart from the cat hairs, it looks almost presentable. Well done!"

Mr. Cassidy dropped the flour baby into the huge double-duty plastic black garbage bag he'd been keeping in his desk for the occasion.

"One!" he said, cheering visibly.

He pointed again.

"Warren."

Warren glanced at Tyrone who, shrugging, reached in the baby carriage to pull out Warren's little sack of flour.

"We'll settle up now, shall we?" Tyrone asked sweetly, deliberately holding Warren's flour baby over the muddy upturned spikes of Philip Brewster's running shoes.

Business was business, after all.

Scowling, Warren dipped his hands deep in his pockets and pulled out enough cash to redeem his flour baby.

"There you are," he said sourly, handing the little sack to Mr. Cassidy.

Mr. Cassidy dumped the flour bag unceremoniously on the scales.

"Lovely," he said. "Right on target!" And tossed it merrily into the garbage bag.

"Next?"

Before it was too late, Tyrone decided to seize the chance to force public payment on some of his most persistent defaulters. He reached in the baby carriage, and dug out Luis Pereira's flour baby. Accepting defeat as graciously as he could, Luis paid up, and took the flour sack to Mr. Cassidy, who weighed it.

"This one's gained a bit of weight," he said. And then he noticed the sandwiches Luis's mother had carefully pinned to its bottom.

"No," he corrected himself, peeling them off and putting the flour sack on the scales again. "Just within limits. *Just.*"

A weak cheer greeted this announcement. By now the general disappointment had begun to fade as, one by one, the occupants of Room 8 came to realize that, even if they didn't get to kick the flour babies around, there was consolation to be found in using Simon as a substitute. All around, his classmates had begun to take advantage of Simon's frozen misery to indulge in a barrage of hisses and jeers.

"Glorious Explosion, eh, Sime?"

"Wait till break!"

"We'll gloriously explode *you!*"

Mr. Cassidy kept on with his weighing, trying to ignore the cross-currents of disaffection and malevolence slewing about him. Not even having most of them in such a bad mood could stop his own spirits rising. As he called out each name, and dumped each flour sack in the shiny black garbage bag, out of sight, he felt a weight dropping from him.

"Who's left?" he called out. "Billy Simms, do I have yours? Yes? Wayne, then."

Wayne brought his flour baby up to the front.

"Looks a little *thin,*" Mr. Cassidy said critically.

He threw the flour baby on the scales. The little steel pointer did its best, but, after a great deal of desperate quivering, all it could manage was to struggle halfway across the scale.

"Three pounds, seven ounces!" Mr. Cassidy was incredulous. "Only three pounds, seven ounces! Do you realize that this thing of yours has lost almost half its body weight?"

Wayne scowled so horribly that even Mr. Cassidy thought better of pursuing the matter.

And that left only one.

"Simon?"

Simon sat tight.

Mr. Cassidy looked up.

"Simon?" he said again.

Still Simon made no move. The boy looked ashen,

Mr. Cassidy thought. Far more upset than could possibly be justified by the ring of hostile whispering around him. The boy was, after all, the most powerful member of the class by far. And fearless, too. If push came to shove, he could probably leave the whole pack of them lying bruised and battered on the pavement around him. So why on earth was he sitting there looking so wretched? Mr. Cassidy peered at him curiously. Could it be that he had truly believed all that nonsense about kicking the flour bags to pieces? Was this the sad snuffing of a glorious dream?

Really, if you thought about things too much, Mr. Cassidy decided, you could become totally unhinged, teaching in Room 8.

"Simon!" he bellowed. "Get yourself and your flour baby up here. Now!"

Like someone in a deep trance, Simon stood up, dug in his school bag and pulled out the flour baby. Like a sleepwalker, he came up to the scales. Reluctantly, he handed her over.

Mr. Cassidy stared.

"What's this?"

Simon forced himself out of his reverie.

"Sir?"

Mr. Cassidy prodded the flour baby. Her bonnet promptly fell off, and she looked up at him at a distinctly rakish angle out of one badly smudged eye.

"What's this?" Mr. Cassidy repeated.

Simon was baffled.

"It's my flour baby, sir."

Mr. Cassidy's look turned to one of dark displeasure.

"But it's *disgusting*," he thundered. "It's utterly revolting. It's in the most disgraceful state. It's an absolute *outrage*."

"She did get a little bit grubby," Simon admitted.

"Little bit grubby?" Mr. Cassidy lifted the flour baby by one of its corners. "This isn't grubby. This is *black*."

"Not exactly *bl* —"

But Mr. Cassidy didn't give him the chance to argue.

"I don't know how you have the nerve to bring this travesty, this *disgrace*, up to my desk." He turned the flour baby over. "And what's all this?" he roared. "Burn! Gum! Mud! Glue! Dribble!"

"It's not *my* dribble, sir," Simon hastened to point out. He was all set to embark on his prepared indictment of Ruggles when he realized it was too late. Mr. Cassidy had reached flashpoint. While everyone else in the room settled back in their seats to relish Simon's discomfiture, Mr. Cassidy leaned over his desk, and stuck his angry face closer.

"I've put up with a good deal from you already," he shouted at Simon. "I've put up with your dark mulligrubs, and your fooling around in Assembly, and your continual persecution of poor Miss Arnott.

But if you think for one moment I am going to put up with being handed back this — this —"

He lifted the flour baby and shuddered.

"This revolting little horror bag —"

He held it over the waste basket.

"Then you are wrong. Quite wrong."

The flour baby trembled in his angry grip as she hung, sagging and disheveled, over whatever sticky remnants of food had recently been spat out under orders.

Simon's eyes widened with panic. He couldn't drop her in there. *Surely* he couldn't.

He could, and did.

In a flash, with one of those lightning moves that kept him on the team, Simon had made the save. As Mr. Cassidy dropped the little sack of flour and turned away in irritation and disgust, Simon's hands shot out and caught it. And with a simultaneous access of quick thinking, he kicked the waste basket, hard.

"There!" Mr. Cassidy said, satisfied at what he took to be the clang of flour baby in waste basket. "Now can we get on with some work, please?"

He picked up a stump of chalk, and started scratching away on the blackboard. Hastily, Simon stuffed the flour baby under his sweatshirt and turned back to face the class. No one seemed to have noticed his sleight of hand and foot. Good. They were all still glaring at him, certainly. But as he stumbled back to his seat, no one reached out and poked or grabbed at the telltale bulge in his sweatshirt. For the moment, she was safe.

Simon collapsed onto his chair, and tried to pay attention to Mr. Cassidy.

"I'm writing names up here," he was telling them sternly. "The names of everyone who still has days missing from his flour baby diary. I don't care if you find them, rewrite them, or make them up. But everyone is to hand in enough for eighteen days."

Not surprisingly, given its length, the list took some time to chalk up on the blackboard. While his classmates were busy watching out for their names, and, by extension, the chance for a noisy and protracted wrangle about the precise number of entries that were actually missing, Simon managed to smuggle his flour baby, completely unnoticed, out from under his sweatshirt into the safe haven of his desk.

Mr. Cassidy wrote the last name — Rick Tullis — up very neatly in the top left-hand corner, well out of the way, since the chances were high it would stay there.

Then he turned around.

"Anyone who finishes," he consoled them, "may go off to the library and do some private study."

The general aura of resentment cleared a little at this announcement. One or two of them even cheered up enough to punch their fists in the air. For most of the occupants of Room 8, the words "private study" were generally taken to be synonymous with "have a good laugh."

Only George O'Rourke still seemed dissatisfied.

"But what about the snoopers?"

"Snoopers?"

"Yes, sir. Aren't you going to tell us who the snoopers were?"

"Snoopers . . ."

A feeling of unease crept over Mr. Cassidy. Snoopers . . . Picking up Dr. Devoy's huge Science Fair memorandum, he turned to the page of rules in order to refresh his memory, and his eye fell on the one claiming that certain people — parents, pupils, staff, or even members of the public — would secretly be checking on the flour babies.

He wasn't supposed to have done anything about that, was he?

Mr. Cassidy turned over a page and saw the number in the top corner — 84. He turned back a page. Number 81. Not the sort of error Dr. Devoy would make. A man who could spin around the school not only correcting the mistakes in everyone else's mental arithmetic, but also pointing out how they came to make the error in the first place, must know how to number pages correctly. Why, even Mr. Cassidy could *count*.

Gently, carefully, fearfully, Mr. Cassidy picked at the uncommonly thick page in question to find that, as he suspected, the hidden pages numbered 82 and 83 peeled apart, revealing detailed instructions for the teacher on the recruitment and supervision of out-of-class observers.

Snapping the memorandum shut, Mr. Cassidy said firmly to George:

"Oh, I don't think we need worry our heads about the snoopers."

George couldn't have disagreed more strongly.

"You have to tell us who they *were*," he insisted. "So we can go out and bash them."

It seemed that, on this issue at least, the whole class was in accord.

"Yes! Punch their lights out!"

"Rearrange their faces!"

"Give them a knuckle sandwich!"

Mr. Cassidy was reduced to cunning.

"I know," he said. "You make a list of everyone you think was snooping on you, and I'll tell you if you're right."

They fell to the task with a will. And Mr. Cassidy was astonished to find each and every one of them laboring to write a list of a dozen or more badly-spelled names, to the accompaniment of a barrage of offensive remarks.

"I'm putting her down first. Nosy bat!"

"Prying old busybody! I don't think she took her beady eyes off me for a moment!"

" 'Trying for your spy badge?' I asked him. 'I don't even know what you're talking about,' he said. But I *knew*. Oh, yes. I *knew*."

Mr. Cassidy ambled around the class, watching in amazement as their lists of suspects grew longer and longer and their mutterings more and more baleful.

It was extraordinary, he thought. And something to tell Dr. Devoy. It was a waste of time recruiting real snoopers. There was clearly no need for that at all.

He walked past Tariq just as the boy was complaining venomously:

"Of course, they claimed they were just taking an interest. Anyone else would call it *meddling*."

And the point was borne out in Billy Simms's last diary entry.

DAY 18

Good thing it's the last day because I couldn't stand any more prying and nagging. People with real babies must be totally soft targets if even flour babies make people you've never even met before come up and pretty well order you around. "I wouldn't leave it there, dear. It might get muddy." "Don't you think you ought to blah-blah-blah." "Shouldn't you blah-blah-blah-blah-bl—"

Mr. Cassidy reached down and lifted Billy Simms's pen off the last *blah*.

"Stuck in a groove?" he asked pleasantly. "Allow me to help you."

Ignoring Billy's poisonous look, he moved on to read Philip Brewster's last effort. Here again, the subject of snoopers was well to the fore.

What got me most about the flour babies was how sneaky people are. They go

*around pretending they're just being friendly
and chatting to you, but really they're telling
you you ought to be doing things differently.
"I'll tell you how I coped with mine," they
say, smiling creepily. Or, "What I found
worked best was this." And you're supposed
to smile back, and pretend you're so thick
you haven't realized that they're telling
you off.*

And Tyrone, as usual, cogently summed up the whole issue.

*I'll tell you what I can't understand. You can
hardly open the newspaper without reading
about someone who's been arrested for
bashing a baby, and it's never the first time
they did it. I don't understand that, really I
don't. I only had to give my flour baby a
look, and my whole family was practically
lining up to phone the police and tell on
me. So where do all these baby bashers
live? Don't they have any family? Don't they
have neighbors? Don't they have any fr —*

Tyrone raised his head.

"How do you spell 'friends'?" he asked of the room at large.

No reason not to try mending a fence or two, Simon thought, and spoke up.

"I think it's f–r–e–i–n–d–s. I wrote it that way a few minutes ago, and it looked all right to me."

Dutifully, Mr. Cassidy strolled across the room to correct Simon's pitiful spelling. But before reaching down to despoil the last diary entry with his marking pen, he stood quietly behind the desk for a few moments, practicing the skilled decoder's art.

DAY 18. OVER & OUT

So I was all wrong about the Glorious Explosion and getting to kick the flour babies to pieces at the end. Who cares? I was planning on cheating anyway. I was going to hide mine, and join in battering everyone else's. I might be in Room 8 but I'm not absolutely stupid. I figured out days ago that I wouldn't be able to hurt mine, not any more, not now that I've grown to like her. (And especially not now, when everyone hates me and I have no fr —

Mr. Cassidy was just leaning over, pen uncapped, to rearrange the next two vowels, when both of them disappeared before his eyes, dissolving in a miniature blue pool.

A teardrop. No doubt about it. And just like everything else about the boy, it was enormous. Hastily, before more could fall, Mr. Cassidy dug in his jacket pocket, fished out the huge spotted handkerchief, and thrust it into Simon's hand.

Simon stared down at the large blue blur on his work. No doubt about it. It was a teardrop. What was the matter with him? If he didn't get a grip, the others might notice. Come break-time, he would be *destroyed*.

Gratefully he took the handkerchief he was offered. And while Mr. Cassidy heaved his massive back end up on Simon's desk, deliberately shielding him from everyone's view, he tried to pull himself together.

When Mr. Cassidy felt the damp handkerchief pushed back in his hand, he took it that it was safe to slide off the desk, and keep on reading.

> I really liked having that flour baby to look after, even though I got sick of her and she drove me berserk. I liked seeing her sitting on top of the dresser watching me while I lay in bed at night. I liked chatting to her at breakfast. And I liked cuddling her to make Ruggles jealous. Last night, when I was rocking her in my arms, Mom said I reminded her of someone. She didn't say who, and I didn't have to ask. But it was good to know he used to rock me like that when I was a baby. Maybe he really did love me, in his way.

Quite forgetting, in the emotion of the moment, that the handkerchief had already been pressed into service more than once, Mr. Cassidy drew it out, and, lighting on a fairly dry patch, blew his nose in a trumpeting fashion. Then, bravely, he forced himself to read to the end.

*He just wasn't very good at showing it,
running away like that. But I can't talk, can
I? My flour baby ended up such a mess, I
practically got my ears torn off. But I really
did care about her. I really did.*

Mr. Cassidy could bear it no longer.

"For heaven's sake, lad," he whispered hoarsely.
"If you love the thing that much, go and fish it out
of the waste basket. Take it home."

Simon said nothing. But, flushing scarlet, he unconsciously leaned forward and gripped the sides of
his desk.

Slowly, suspiciously, Mr. Cassidy tipped Simon
back a few inches, lifted the desk lid, and peered in.

The flour baby peered back at him anxiously, out
of the dark.

Mr. Cassidy lowered the desk lid. He looked at
Simon. Simon looked at him. Then Mr. Cassidy said:

"Do you want to know your problem, Simon
Martin? You sell yourself too short. Your flour
baby is a squalid and disgusting little creature. She
wouldn't pass any hygiene tests, and, if she were real,
she wouldn't win any Natty Baby competitions. But
if keeping what you care for close and safe counts for
anything, I'll tell you this. You'll make a better father
than most."

Then, clearing his throat loudly, he strode off as
fast as he could, back to the sanctuary of his own
desk.

CHAPTER 10

Fired with determination to get the whole flour baby project out of the way for good, Mr. Cassidy kept everyone working. And as the clock hand rolled around the hour, interminably slowly, the sense of righteous outrage always felt by the occupants of Room 8 when sustained effort was expected of them merged with their resentment of Simon for his two terrible mistakes: picking the project in the first place, and being wrong about the glorious explosion.

For form's sake, Mr. Cassidy pretended he was deaf to the flurries of malignant whispering around him.

"What sort of *Warpo* chooses to do babies anyhow?"

"We could have chosen *any* of the other ones. We could have done *food.*"

To try and distract them, he picked up the sheet of paper Spike Moranis had just pushed aside with a huge sigh of relief.

"Here. Someone's finished. Let me inspire the rest of you by reading out Spike's final entry."

He held it in front of his eyes for a few moments, trying — and failing — to decipher it.

"You're holding it upside down," Spike said reproachfully.

Hastily, Mr. Cassidy turned the page the other way up.

"Ah, yes!" he said. "That's better."

He peered at it for a few moments longer, concentrating hard, and then, defeated, gave it back to Spike.

"I wonder if you haven't been just a shade overambitious," he suggested gently. "Trying to move on to cursive writing quite so soon."

As he stepped away, the bell rang, precipitating the usual frenzy of illicit bag-packing and chair-scraping.

"Wait till the voice goes green!" he roared.

The squall abated for a moment.

Mr. Cassidy decided to make for the teachers' room, and his reviving cup of coffee, a few minutes ahead of the stampede. Imposing his will on the entire class with the darkest of looks, he moved backward to the door. Then,

"Now," he said. "Off you go."

Before the words were even out of his mouth, he was away, down the long corridor.

With authority gone, the pack instantly went after their true quarry.

"Thought you could get away with it, did you, Sime?"

"Leading us on like that!"

" 'Best science I've ever heard,' you told us. 'Terrific! Unbeatable!' you said."

Once again, Simon unconsciously leaned forward and gripped his desk. No one believed the gesture stemmed from fear, and so for the second time that morning it proved his undoing.

"What have you got in there?"

"Open up, Sime!"

"Let's see!"

They were too many for him. Their combined weight, and the enthusiastic charge, toppled the desk and sent the lid flying open.

The flour baby shot out and sailed over the energetically fighting mob. She flew high over the abandoned desks. Simon skidded beneath, tracking her flight, and managed to catch her, puffing flour from every pore, just as Mr. Cassidy came back to fetch his cigarettes.

Striding to his desk, Mr. Cassidy took a brief, irritable look at the disorder and the small cloud of flour settling on the far side of the room. After wasting time retracing his steps, he wasn't in the mood to fritter away more of his precious break pursuing either truth or justice.

It was Simon he blamed.

"Monday detention!" he boomed. "For starting an unruly ball game in my classroom."

Lifting the desk lid a few inches, he surreptitiously drew the telltale cigarette package out from its hiding place under some papers in the corner. Then, seeing that they were all trying to work out why he'd come back, he made a show of grasping the huge plastic bag of flour babies and dragging it out of the door behind him.

Simon stood staring at his departing back, outraged by the sheer injustice of the punishment. Sensing his temporary loss of concentration, Wayne dived for the flour baby. Without thinking twice, Simon spun around and hurled her in the air, giving himself enough time to leap on the seat of a chair, catch her safely, and hold her out of Wayne's reach.

Hearing the scuffle from halfway down the corridor, Mr. Cassidy strode back and caught Simon standing on the chair.

"Tuesday detention!" he bellowed. "For climbing on school property."

Again, he turned to go.

Simon stood, encircled and besieged, as the rest of the class crept closer, bent on the capture of his flour baby. Should he leap for the door now, before they expected him to make a move? They knew as well as he did that Mr. Cassidy would hear him pounding the other way down the corridor, whip around, and give him yet another detention for running within the school building.

But so what? Marooned on his chair, holding the flour baby high, Simon couldn't help thinking it. So *what?* There were worse things in life than getting three detentions in a row. Why, even added up, they wouldn't last longer than one of Hyacinth Spicer's grisly birthday parties, and he'd survived seven of those.

So maybe he should just go for it. Give it a whirl. What had Old Hopalong said: "*Aren't you supposed to be one of the school's athletic heroes?*"

Yes, go for it!

In a rush of exhilaration, Simon suddenly astonished everyone around him by leaping for the door. The noise was tremendous. From desk to desk he leaped, leaving wobbly wooden legs rattling frantically, and chairs keeling over backwards. He held the flour baby high, and, as he jumped, what Mr. Cassidy said rang in his ears. "*Do you want to know your problem, Simon Martin? You sell yourself too short.*" He sprang from Wayne's desk to Spike's in a clatter of flying pens and rulers. He sent Philip Brewster's calculator flying. He vaulted over Luis's desk entirely. And with one last tremendous bound, he made it to safety. He was through the door, punching the air with a fist. He felt as powerful as when, all those years ago, Miss Ness pinned the wonderful scarlet cloak around him for the nativity play, and he could practically hear trumpets. Who'd make a bad father? Not him, for sure. Maybe people like Robin Delaney couldn't stand the pace, and ended up putting an early end to their responsibilities. And people like Sue never even dared risk it. But as for him, Simon Martin, he wouldn't be bad at all. In fact, he'd be *better* than not bad. He'd be pretty *good*. In a glorious, glorious explosion of confidence, the words Mr. Cassidy said echoed mightily in his brain: "*If keeping what you care for close and safe counts for anything, you'll make a better father than most.*"

The foot stuck out to trip him brought him down. He landed with a thud and a grunt, and lay, spread-eagled and winded, as the flour baby shot out of his hands, and slid twenty feet along the corridor.

The real voice put instant flight to the echo.

"Ah! Simon Martin! Just the boy I need. Wednesday detention, of course, for running in the corridor. But, since you're here, would you be so good as to drag this bag along to Dr. Devoy's Science Fair? That's a good lad."

And, patting the comforting little package in his jacket pocket, Mr. Cassidy hurried off for his coffee and a quick smoke.

Simon had just hauled himself painfully into a sitting position when Dr. Devoy spun around the corner with a bevy of helpers in tow, carrying the various parts of the Lescher twins' hydroelectric power station.

"Back! Back, back, back!" Like a lion tamer, Dr. Devoy snarled at the pack of boys fighting their way through the doorway after Simon. "Get back! Back at once! Can't you see this is expensive equipment?"

No sooner had he said the words "expensive equipment" than he noticed Wishart's Digital Sine-Wave

Generator on the floor where, on Mr. Cassidy's orders, Simon had abandoned it earlier.

"What on earth?"

Then he saw the oscilloscope lying beside the radiator.

"This is outrageous!"

Then he saw Simon.

"You! You there, boy! Lounging about on the floor! You!"

Aware of the crippling limitations of speech, Simon simply hung his head.

"Monday detention!" Dr. Devoy ordered.

"I'm booked up till Wednesday," Simon told him sourly.

"Thursday, then!" snapped Dr. Devoy. "Now look sharp! That equipment should have been taken down to the laboratories well over an hour ago."

Sighing, Simon scrambled to his feet, and looked around for someone to help him. But everyone from Room 8 had disappeared. Simon presumed, bitterly and rightly, that they had prudently begun to melt away the instant Dr. Devoy started firing on all cylinders and dishing out punishment detentions. So taking off only a moment to make a horrible face at his tormentor's back, Simon thrust his own flour baby safely back under his sweatshirt, and gathered up Wishart's Digital Sine-Wave Generator and the oscilloscope. After shifting them around a little, he managed to find a way of carrying both that left a few fingers free. With these, he grasped the neck of the heavy-duty garbage bag, and, slowly, slowly, stumbled backwards along the corridor, still balancing the equipment in his arms.

He found Mr. Cianelli standing in wait behind the third set of swinging doors in the science block.

"About time!" He snatched the oscilloscope from Simon. "This should have been here well over an hour ago!"

He consulted the massive Science Fair display plan Dr. Devoy had pinned to the wall.

"That thing of Wishart's goes in here as well."

As he lifted the Digital Sine-Wave Generator out of Simon's arms, he noticed the third and last burden.

"What's in that garbage bag?"

"Flour babies."

Mr. Cianelli took another look at the master plan.

"Flour babies . . . flour babies . . . Ah! Here we are!" His face crumpled into a frown. "*Early,* aren't they? Oh, never mind. Display on Table 18."

In vain he waited for Simon to make a move.

"Go on, then," he repeated impatiently. "Go and display them."

Simon scowled. He was sick of people snapping at him.

"How?" he asked sullenly.

But Mr. Cianelli had a bigger fish to fry. Pitkin's Electronic Window Burglar Alarm was just being carried through the door.

"For heaven's sake, boy!" he scolded Simon. "Do you have to be *spoon-fed?* Just set the things out to look interesting, and write a label explaining what they are."

So Simon grudgingly dragged the huge black bag over to Table 18, which, he couldn't help noticing with a flicker of resentment, was the one hidden away farthest in the corner. He pulled out the flour babies one by one, and dumped them on the table. Looking at each in turn, he was aware for the first time how much most of them had changed over the last eighteen days. His was no longer the only one with eyes. Several had noses, ears, lips, and even warts. George O'Rourke's appeared to have measles. Billy Simms's sported one of his specialty bluebottle tattoos. Luis's even had a pipe.

Now what would make an interesting display?

First, Simon pulled his own flour baby out from under his sweatshirt and set her in the middle of the table. Then he put all the others in a circle around her.

Good.

He took a label from a nearby table and turned it over to the blank side.

"*Queen Flour Baby and Her Courtiers,*" he wrote, then looked at it critically. Even if people could make out what it said, they wouldn't find it interesting.

He tried again. This time he divided the flour babies into pairs, and tried to set them in the sorts of positions that suggested a Saturday night party.

He stole the card from another table. Crossing out the neatly printed words *Measuring the Wavelength of Laser Light,* he turned it over and tried to write:

Orgy.

Only four letters, and yet he suspected that at least two of them were wrong, or badly out of place. And, anyway, it didn't look like a very interesting party. He tried to liven it up a bit by moving the flour babies into more interesting positions. But somehow they still managed to persist in looking disappointingly like eighteen little sacks of flour, just lying in a jumble on the table.

Giving up, Simon tried something different. This time he set them out in strict rows and wrote "*Dr. Devoy's Class of Earholes*" on yet another card.

Not very interesting.

His next idea was the best. Taking the card belonging to Hocking's Zero Gravity Project, he wrote on the back: "*Simon Martin's Greatest Goal Ever.*" And then he set to re-creating it with the help of the flour babies and a chocolate bar wrapper he found on the floor and crumpled up for a soccer ball.

First he put the front three players into place. Then the middle four, and then the back three. Then he put in the other team. He'd played deep in defense, that glorious day. But when the time came, he'd dribbled the ball up the wing in an astonishing spurt of speed, swerving to miss one defender after another. He'd reached the edge of the penalty area, and let fly such a kick that the ball shot straight in the corner of the net. The goalie didn't even see it, and Simon didn't have the time to swing away from the inevitable collision with their beefy, cross-eyed sweeper.

Taken up with the memory, he ran through the last moves of play, propelling the flour babies.

"Baroom! Baroom! Pow!"

As the two sacks collided, flour puffed out and showered all over.

Out of the way the table might have been. Invisible it wasn't. Mr. Cianelli had stormed over within seconds.

"Flour! You're getting flour over everything! What's the matter with you, Simon Martin? Why are you acting even more like a halfwit than usual?"

Simon was nettled. He had, after all, only been doing his best to follow orders.

Mr. Cianelli spun around like a frenzied top.

"Look!" he was shouting. "Look at all this flour! It's settling on Bernstein's Pressurized Cylinders! And Butterworth's Speech Synthesis machine! You can take a detention for this, Simon Martin."

"Friday's my earliest," Simon informed him in a voice that was icy with resentment.

"Friday, then! And don't think I won't be in to check on you. I'll —"

Mr. Cianelli broke off.

"My God! Now it's drifting down into Rawson's Purified Water apparatus!"

He turned on Simon.

"Get those things out of here!"

"But —"

"Get them out!"

Mr. Cianelli was in such a fury that Simon didn't

argue. Hastily, he shoveled all the flour babies, including his own, into the garbage bag.

"Hurry up! Quick! Get them out of here! Take them away!"

Still scowling, Simon dragged the bag toward the door.

"But where should I —?"

Mr. Cianelli was in no mood to solve Simon's problem.

"Just get them out! Take them away! I don't care if you kick the damn things to pieces. Just get them out of this building! Now!"

Obediently, Simon dragged the heavy bag out of the door and back past the other laboratories. He was in no mood to take care going through the swinging doors, and the bag snagged on one set of floor catches after another. The trail of flour he was leaving behind grew wider and deeper with each step.

He'd reached the main door out of the science block when he ran into Miss Arnott.

"What are you doing out of class?" she asked. "The bell rang for the end of break several minutes ago."

Simon considered. He could claim that he was taking the flour babies to the science block. But it was unlikely that Miss Arnott would believe him, since he was clearly heading the other way.

He could claim he was taking them back to his own classroom. But she was more than capable of watching until he'd gone through the door. And, like messengers of old who brought bad news and were killed for their pains, Simon seriously doubted the wisdom of being the one to bring the flour babies back to Mr. Cassidy.

Or he could say nothing, as usual.

He said nothing, as usual.

Miss Arnott patted her shoulder bag to check that she still had her bottle of aspirin with her.

"I'm sorry, Simon, but I have no choice. If you don't have a reason to be out of class, I'm forced to give you a detention."

"It will have to be a week from Monday," Simon warned her. "I'm fully booked till then."

"Oh, Simon!" said Miss Arnott, pressing the points on her temples where her headaches always started.

"It's all right," Simon assured her valiantly. "I don't mind." And it was true. Between trying to explain, and taking another detention, he much preferred the detention. It was easier.

"A week from Monday, then."

Like an unseasonal Santa, Simon nodded, gripped the large plastic bag, and moved off grimly down the corridor. Miss Arnott stepped aside to let him pass.

And saw the trail of flour.

"Simon —"

"Yes, Miss Arnott?"

But she had gone, fleeing to the teachers' room to get some water for her aspirin. Simon stood looking at her footprints down the flour. Something — call it prescience, call it second sight — warned him Miss Arnott wouldn't be with them very much longer. The woman was losing her grip, that was quite obvious. And if there was one thing you needed to be a teacher, it was grip. You needed it from a quarter past eight in the morning till quarter past four at night. He stopped to count the hours on his fingers. Eight. It sounded a major grind, but, when you came to think, it was only a third of each day. Eight measly hours. If poor Miss Arnott couldn't even manage that, then she'd better not quit and have a baby.

Now there was a *real* job, thought Simon. Twenty-four-hour shifts. Every day. For nearly twenty years. No breaks. No holidays. It made one of Hyacinth's parties look like a mayfly's quick blink. Being a parent was pretty well a life sentence. Why, if instead of going off to the hospital to have a baby all those years ago, his mother had stabbed someone to death with a bread knife, she'd be out of jail by now. Twice over, probably, if she'd been good.

Simon tugged his own flour baby out of the garbage bag and stared at her. The more you thought about it, the more extraordinary it was, this business of having babies. No doubt about it, it was dangerous. It slowed you up. It tied you down. It cramped your style. It brought out the spy and the nag in everyone around you. And it made being a teacher look like party time. No wonder his father hadn't been able to stick it. How had he even lasted a thousand and eight hours? That was twice as long as

Simon had taken care of his flour baby. And look at his mother! Her score was up in the hundreds of thousands already! She must be a real *heroine*. She must be a *saint*.

"She must be absolutely sick of me," he told the flour baby.

But it wasn't true, and he knew it. The words even rang a little hollowly down the corridor. Because Simon knew in his heart that, give or take the occasional days when he'd done something truly half-witted like feeding Grandma's wig to Tullis's German shepherd, or throwing that cactus at Hyacinth, she was really quite fond of him. That was the problem.

"That's how the trap works," he explained to the flour baby. "That's how it gets you. First you know nothing. Then it's far too late."

He paused.

"Unless you're a tall ship."

A tall ship . . .

His father . . .

Simon sat down on the garbage bag, which bulged voluptuously beneath his weight, and formed a snug nest around him. He was thinking hard.

His father.

Experimentally, he rolled the words out, considering them in a new way.

"My father. My father. My father."

Who?

Who?

"*Who?*"

The live echo was Robin, sent to track him down, and bring him back for a roasting.

"Exactly!" said Simon. "*Who?*"

But Robin was in no mood for riddles. He was on a mission.

"Out of that bag, Sime. Time to get back to base. Old Hopalong is smoldering in his socks."

"You see," explained Simon, ignoring him totally, "I don't know who he is. And he doesn't know who I am. And so what Mom and Grandma say is absolutely true. The fact that he walked out is really nothing to do with me."

"Out of the bag, Sime! Time's up!"

"I'm not saying what he did was *right*," Simon went on. "Sailing off like that and leaving my mom to take care of me forever and ever." He poked the flour baby. "Though after lugging this thing about for three weeks, I can understand how it happened. I'm just saying that it shouldn't — doesn't — matter to me any longer."

"Yes, Sime. Now out of the bag, *please*."

"You see, I'm finished with him," Simon persisted. "In fact, in a way, we never even started. He's really nothing at all to do with me. And out there in the world there are millions and millions of people who have nothing to do with me, who don't even know me. They all get on perfectly well without me. And I get on perfectly well without them."

But Robin's patience had run out.

"Sime, I'm not getting in trouble for you. I'm going back now. I'm going to tell Mr. Cassidy I found you but you wouldn't come. You were too busy sitting in a flour bag, spouting about your family."

It was as if Simon didn't even hear him.

"And what I've realized is that my father is just one more person on the planet who doesn't know who I am. That's all he is. And only the people who know you really count."

"*I'm* counting, Sime."

"And so my mother counts. And Grandma. And Sue."

"One . . ."

"But not him. He doesn't count."

"Two . . ."

"Not that I'm blaming him. But he doesn't count."

"Three!"

Despairing of forcing Simon to see sense, Robin turned to go back to the classroom. And as he reached the bend in the corridor, he could still hear faintly, from behind, the sound of Simon holding forth to his flour baby.

"I feel a lot better now, I really do. I don't think I knew how much the whole business has been bothering me. But I feel different now. I feel *free*."

The flour baby stared back out of her sympathetic, long-lashed eyes.

"You do *see*, don't you?"

The look on her face never altered.

"You *understand?*"

The flour baby watched him impassively.

And slowly, inexorably, Simon came back to his senses. What was he *doing*, sitting in a school corridor in a nice comfy garbage bag, chatting to a lump of flour? Was he *cracked?*

Simon leaped to his feet as if he'd been scalded. Flour baby! She wasn't a flour baby. She was a silly, lifeless bag of flour. She wasn't even a *she*. She was an *it*. What was the *matter* with him? For nearly three weeks now, he'd been discussing his life with a flour sack. Was he *crazy?* This thing he was holding was nothing more than part of some boring school project. She wasn't real. *None* of them were real.

Grasping the corners of the huge garbage bag, he upended it forcibly. Flour sacks spilled far and wide. That's all they were. Flour sacks! Sacks of flour!

Picking one up, he hurled it at the ceiling. It split, showering flour all over. Simon didn't care. He felt the most extraordinary relief, as if he'd suddenly been let out of jail; as if, swimming hopelessly around and around after a shipwreck, he'd spotted lights on land; as if the doctor and the priest and the teacher had come to tell him they were wrong, just a mistake, he wasn't going to have to be a parent yet after all.

It was all over. The relief of it! He hurled another flour baby. And another. Because it had been a near thing, a very near thing. He'd really grown to love his flour baby. He'd really cared about her. But she wasn't real! And so he was free! Free, free, *free!*

The next flour baby caught on the light fixture and tore. Ecstatically, Simon lifted his face to the cascade of flour spilling back on him, and hurled the next flour baby harder. Why should he care? Hadn't Mr. Cianelli all but given him permission, after all? "*I don't care if you kick the damn things to pieces. Just get them out of here.*" And Simon had.

Kick them to pieces, though?

Great idea!

He kicked one, and then another. Flour exploded all over. It billowed down the corridor in mushrooming white clouds. Each time he kicked another flour sack, more huge puffs of pure white transformed the dull corridor into a storm of snow, a dazzling blizzard — a glorious, glorious explosion.

The flour was drifting up the walls, and settling ankle-deep. Who cared? Not huge, white, flour-kicking Simon. There would be time enough to be responsible when he was older. When the right moment came, there would be all the time in the world to be a good father.

But not now. Not while he was so young. Not while he had the strength and power and energy to do anything, and all his horizons were giddy and bright, and wider than he could imagine.

Boot . . . Boot . . . As flour flurried and swirled in arctic chaos, Simon raised his arms to it in triumph. He wouldn't make the same mistake as his father. Oh, no. He wasn't going to pin himself down years too soon, and have to make the bitter choice between snatching back his own life, and leaving some child to dawdle down Revere Street every day, talking inside his head to some crinkly blue-eyed father he'd had to make up all by himself, because the real one hadn't stayed around.

He'd never do that. Never, never, never. He'd wait until he was ready. He'd take care. And then, one day maybe, when he felt like it . . .

Boot . . . Boot . . .

Flour rained on him. It ran all over him in rills and rivulets. It swirled all about him. He was a snowman, a yeti, a walking avalanche. *Boot . . . Boot . . .* He took all the petty frustrations of three weeks out on the tattered bags of flour. "Don't leave her there, Sime." "Be careful." "Are you sure she's safe?" Is this what his mother was feeling all those years ago, when she dragged him down the club so she could let fly playing tennis one measly hour a week? How *could* he have leaned over the balcony nagging at her like that? How *could* he?

Boot . . . Boot . . . Boot . . . More bags split and showered flour. His mother was a *saint.* He'd take her flowers. He'd bully Tyrone into lending some of his ill-gotten gains, and he'd take his mom a dozen red roses. She deserved them.

Simon dipped his arms elbow deep in flour, and, ripping the last few flour babies apart at the seams, he shook the flour all over. He was so happy, nothing could spoil it. They could give him detentions till hell froze. He didn't care. An hour a day? Chicken feed! Look at what he'd just escaped!

He couldn't help it. He burst into song.

"Unfurl the sail, lads, and let the winds find me
Breasting the soft, sunny, blue rising main —"

The strong voice rang out in the storm of flour. Scooping up more handfuls, he tossed them around him, white on white. Oh, lucky, lucky Simon!

"Toss all my burdens and woes clear behind me," he caroled.

"Vow I'll not carry those cargoes again."

The flour gusted around him like a good sou'wester.

"Sail for a sunrise that burns with new maybes —" Louder and louder he sang. He wasn't trapped. He would be punished, but he wasn't trapped. And there'd be time enough to be responsible.

"Farewell, my loved ones, and be of good cheer."

There weren't many scraps of burlap left now. The flour spread all the way down to the corner. It was a pity about there being nothing at all from Room 8 in the Science Fair. Still, never mind. At least they'd learned a lot.

The matchless voice soared.

"Others may settle to dandle their babies —"

With one last kick at the flour, Simon set off down the corridor.

"My heart's a tall ship, and high winds are near."

Martin Simon, taking the opportunity of a trip to the lavatories to finish the last pages of *The Quest for the Holy Grail,* lifted his head from the words he was reading.

"*Here is the source of valor undismayed,*" he couldn't help repeating, whispering it softly to himself. For it did seem that here in front of him was someone magically tall and strong, who walked like a knight in his aura of pure white — awesome and amazing.

Martin Simon flattened himself against the wall as Simon Martin strode past, singing.

And Mr. Cassidy, testily making his way along the corridor to fetch his errant pupil, heard the glorious, glorious tenor voice echoing from ceiling and walls, and fell back respectfully to let the young vision in white sail past, like a tall ship, out into his unfettered youth.

Also available by Anne Fine in a Laurel-Leaf edition

There's something about Tulip. Natalie is drawn to her from the day they meet. The other kids at school are afraid of Tulip, who comes from an abusive family, but Natalie can't resist her deviant charm. It's exciting spending time with Tulip. She can tell a lie so elaborate and outrageous, you want to believe it even though you know it isn't true. People call it "The Tulip Touch."

And nobody thinks up games like Tulip's. They start out rather innocent. Stinking Mackerel. Road of Bones. Hogs in a Tunnel. But soon the games become more complicated—and more dangerous. Natalie knows she must do something to break free of Tulip's spell. But does she have the strength to save herself . . . and Tulip?

Now available wherever books are sold

ISBN: 0-440-22785-2